The Element

by

NATALIE BROUGHAM

Wild Ink Publishing LLC

A Wild Ink Publishing Publishing Original
Wild Ink Publishing
wild-ink-publishing.com

ISBN: 978-1-958531-54-9

This book is dedicated to the love of my life,
my daughter Annabelle.

For all the purpose, strength, and love you
have brought to my life I hope this book
brings you joy in return.

May you always believe in your own power to
create magic.

With all my love,
Mama

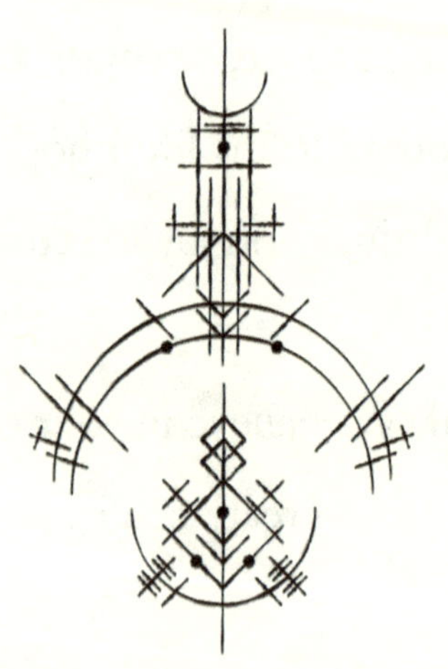

The grass was damp, soaking through Alowen's shirt a bit as she lay flat, staring absently. The sun was so warm on her back she hardly noticed the coolness of the ground. Two feet away, a train of black ants wound around in an indiscernible labyrinth pattern. How they stayed in such precise formation was beyond her.

A breeze rustled the branches of a blossom tree overhead and suddenly sunbeams covered the ground, shining like bits of polished mirror. She closed her eyes and imagined each blade of grass was one of the trees in the Arbor and each ant one of its citizens. How many times had she played this game since she was little? The tiny society the ants lived in felt safe, small, and predictable. She liked that. Lately, life was changing too quickly. She would be graduating soon and the future loomed large before her.

The afternoon spring winds had begun to make her long for summer nights. As she rolled onto her back, looking at the sky through the leaves, a few pink blossoms drifted down around her into her black hair. One of them floated from the tree right into the palm of her hand. She held it gently. It was moments like this where she felt so deeply in love with the Arbor she couldn't imagine being anywhere else.

Alowen had only ever known the Arbor. The country-side may not be as loud as Bachha, the fire city, or mysterious as Allurus, where Water People dwelt, or ornate as the Sky People's mountain city Wolken, but the Arbor had sown stronger people amongst the Frozen Years generations ago. That harsh winter that stretched entire lifetimes had seen its heartiest, bravest hunters, and its communities had never seen petty division. It was home for her and those who are deeply connected to the Earth. It smelled of wood fires and soft, damp grass. There were rumors that fairies lived here. The brick walls of shops had tiny doors built into them where children could leave their wishes. Nothing was more gratifying than sitting on a hill at night and watching the sun bow out of the sky, leaving trails of magenta and burnt orange behind, falling to the Earth. You would swear you'd never seen that shade of purple anywhere else in the Universe. These were the things that made up Alowen, the things she would carry with her the rest of her life.

The pit of her stomach twinged. She would carry these images with her. But she would also carry her grief. All of these things reminded her that her father wasn't here. Her father had died when she was only three. Her memories of him were blurry. The sound of his ringing laugh that shook the walls, his warmth when he held her small body to his chest, his smell of chopped wood and crisp autumn air were all gone now, and she ached to know why. She had already inspected every blade of grass, every creek, every baby turtle around the Arbor, and still, she didn't know so many things. Alowen knew she couldn't stay here forever, but her palms ached with grief when she thought of leaving.

"Alowen!"

She groaned softly.

Her mother's voice called her to help with dinner. It could get enraging whenever she insisted Alowen stop daydreaming and put an hour or two into the business of the real world. If the world was made of two types of people, she was the type that needed answers. Her mother was the type who held things together by insisting answers weren't necessary and that making stew and washing clothes were much more important to the unfolding of the universe than answering silly philosophical questions about the existence of life in the first place.

Still, Alowen was lucky to have such a strong, dedicated woman for a mother, especially with her father gone. She had a presence that made the world seem safe, fair, even reasonable. She believed the world to be that way, and so it was.

Lazily, she shifted to sit up. "Coming!"

She lifted herself from the soft ground and walked slowly through the grass. Lately, she hadn't been hungry. It was as though her mind was already far in the future. Her uncle was coming to dinner this evening with a "surprise" for her. With school coming to an end, she had a few ideas of what it could be. Most people around Alowen knew she dreamed of seeing other places and being a writer famous for pointing out lovely pieces of the world no one else saw.

There was Astara Institute, a writing school in Wolken, the most famous city in sky country. Unfortunately, her mother didn't have the money to send her, so maybe her uncle would bring news he would pay for her to attend. She quickened her steps at the thought.

The smell of warm biscuits baking greeted her as she opened the front door. Her mother looked up from the kitchen counter where she was carving a freshly roasted chicken. Her long auburn hair was tucked up and pinned carefully out of her face as usual.

"Alowen, there you are. Bring me that bag of carrots, please. That sweet boy Mikal came and left them for us." She hummed softly as her knife sawed up and down.

Alowen forced down a tug of nausea. Mikal was bright and handsome with thick blond hair and a smile that could sell milk to a dairy farm. He was one of the Arbor's most popular boys. He was also very openly pursuing Alowen's hand in marriage, even though she had told him she was not interested. Apparently, it only compelled him to try harder. He became more handsome, muscular, and competitive with each passing year, all to break down Alowen's resistance and secure her as his. It was embarrassing how her mother knew about his feelings. The Arbor was big enough that everyone knew almost everyone—and almost all their business as well.

"Did you hear me, dear? You must be sure to thank Mikal." Her mom, of course, thought it was wonderful Alowen had such a handsome boy pursuing her and she wouldn't hear a word of it when her daughter argued he was as dense as a Wolkenian fog. "His father's harvest did so well this year and it's very kind of them to share their good fortune with us."

"Right"—Alowen nodded stiffly as she placed the bag of carrots closer—"I will be sure to, Mom." Time to change the subject. "So, when will Uncle Rogan be here? I want to wash up before he arrives."

Her mother glanced distractedly at the clock. "I'm not sure, dear. Soon though. He said he was bringing someone with him; didn't say who. He was in a terrible hurry; you know Rogan."

A mystery guest? Alowen excused herself to her room. Her mind raced as she flung dresses onto the bed. Could this be what Uncle Rogan had mentioned? What could a guest have to do with her surprise? Regardless, she needed to be presentable. She slipped a lavender cotton dress over her head and glanced at her mirror. Thankfully, she had her mom's pretty green eyes, especially stark against her dad's black hair. She pinched her cheeks to make them flush. Alright, show time.

Just as she stepped out, there was a knock on the door.

"Please get that, honey. I have my hands full." Her mother was looking over several simmering pots at once.

The smell of roasted chicken and biscuits made Alowen ravenous. The plate of vegetables almost looked like a rainbow with carrots, red and green peppers, purple onions, and red potatoes all drenched in butter. She put on her least surprised expression before she opened the door expectantly. She hated anyone catching her off guard. But it was just Uncle Rogan. She tried not to look disappointed.

"You look lovely, Alowen!" She squealed as he scooped her off the floor and spun. Her uncle had been doing that since she was a very little girl, and it still made her giggle. "Hello, Eliza! Wow, it smells like you have done it again. Frazyk has never had a meal like this before, I'm sure."

The color left both their faces. Alowen began frantically pinching her cheeks to bring back the flush.

"Frazyk?!" Her mother spun, splattering gravy from the spoon in her hand which she now pointed menacingly at Rogan. "You invited the Mayor of Wolken to my house for dinner without any warning!?" She approached him, and he backed against the door trying to deflect the gravy with his hands.

"Eliza, it will be fine! He is a friend, and he is very down to Earth. He is only here to have a casual meal and meet both of you. So just relax, alright?" Alowen's mother shot him a glower.

"Better grab a rag and wipe this mess up. I'm getting an apron with less flour on it, and I don't want to see any splotches when I'm done."

Eliza hurried to change aprons as Uncle Rogan wiped away the mess and rolled his eyes mock-annoyedly at Alowen, whose cheeks were perfectly flush again.

"Alowen, I didn't tell you before because I didn't want you to be nervous. He is here to interview you to be a scribe for this year's Element Party!"

The color drained from Alowen's cheeks and back down to her toes. This time she could think of nothing but what Uncle Rogan just said.

"The Element Party?" It sounded like a small mouse crawled inside her mouth and squeaked out the question. The Element Party was the biggest event of the year, held in the fire city of Bachha—the hub of all four worlds. Every famous person of any Element spent most of their time there, from philosophical Sky People, imaginative Fire People, and mysterious Water People. And amidst all of that could be her, from the humble Arbor.

But Baccha thrived all night long. It may as well, the city was encased in an enormous shell under the sea, lit by the strange glow of fire bouncing off its pearly walls. It gave the impression of always seeing through a rosy haze. Every year, four young, promising citizens were chosen to represent each Element and record the events of the party, which were so legendary many people only ever dreamed about attending. Everyone dressed in lavish gowns and costumes. Performers took up every corner, entertaining crowds with extravagant songs and magic. That wasn't even the last of it if rumors could be believed.

Only those who went knew what really happened. The selected party scribes were assured a prestigious career in their chosen field. Many went on to become correspondents for high council, mediators, and recorders of history. This was it. Her chance was finally here and all she wanted to do was run to her room and hide. No, she wouldn't ruin this.

What did she have to lose?

As if on cue, there was a loud tap on the door. She jumped, composing her hair and cotton dress.

"Rogan!" Her mother motioned to her uncle to open the door.

As soon as it opened, a large hand with long thin fingers appeared around the doorframe, and in stepped the tallest man she had ever seen. His hair was stark silver with spiky tips that lightly brushed the ceiling. He wore a long purple cape over a robe that shone as it caught the light as though it were made of liquid. His skin looked strange too, almost iridescent, and his eyes seemed to change from pale blue to yellow and back as he moved about in the light. His features were delicate, almost feminine, but the total effect was pleasing, if not slightly overwhelming. Around his wrist was the standard glass bracelet all Wolkenians wore to keep their natural telepathy from invading other people's minds without permission. He smiled around the room expectantly.

"Frazyk, so glad to have you!" Rogan grabbed him by the arm and pulled him into a hug that seemed to make breathing difficult. "This is my brother's widow, Eliza, and her daughter, my niece Alowen."

Alowen curtsied as her mother blushed and shook his hand.

"I've left my transportation in the yard. Do you think the neighbors will mind?"

Something dark and huge shifted outside, blotting away the remaining daylight through the window. Alowen peered out to see an eagle as large as a cow looking hungrily toward the chicken coop. It stretched its wings, ruffling bronze and grey feathers, and she flinched as it angled a gleaming eye into the house. "If I may?" Mayor Frazyk reached into a robe pocket and slid out a bloody flank of meat.

"Oh no! Heaven's mercy, no. We have animals running

wild all over the farms in the Arbor! They couldn't possibly mind," Alowen's mother said nervously.

Frazyk opened the window and tossed the meat into the eagle's beak, then wiped his hands on a towel Uncle Rogan offered.

"Thank you, friend. I'll get that." He closed the window again.

What an intimidating animal, Alowen thought. She'd heard about the people of Wolken and their eccentric choice of transportation but had never seen a giant eagle up close.

Her mother clapped her hands together, bringing her back to the room. "Well, I'm sure you are starving, Mayor Frazyk! Does it take an awfully long time to get to the Arbor from Wolken? Oh no, no. Alowen will take that for you; you have a seat. I am going to fetch you a biscuit and some chicken." Her mother nodded sharply at her, and she hastily grabbed the purple cloak, ushering Frazyk to a chair at the head of the table.

The mayor smiled curiously at her as he eased himself down.

"Time? No, not really. Although I tend to lose track when I am traveling." His smile now turned to a smirk. Alowen could have sworn he winked in her direction. "What have you prepared tonight? I must say the smell is overwhelming. I hadn't realized how famished I was."

"Well, it's nothing really, just whatever we had around the farm." Alowen's mother shot Rogan an icy stare. "If my brother-in-law had informed me we were having such an important guest, I would have made sure we had something more suitable."

"No need for flattery, Eliza." Frazyk's curious smile seemed fixed. "There is nothing so important about a mayor. I really just run the meetings. Don't tell anyone I said this, but I have loads of free time. Tyrq and I spend our time just coasting the air drafts!" He chuckled and grabbed the jug of berry wine on the table.

Outside, the massive eagle threw its head back and swallowed the slab of meat whole.

"Tyrq? Your … er… transportation?" Her mother seemed unsure how to address such a celebrity who seemed to think nothing much of himself.

"Oh, hmmm?" Frazyk glanced up from his soup spoon. "Yes, ahh see sometimes I forget myself. Tyrq has become quite infamous in Wolken. We have taken to dropping down behind some of the less humble citizens just to remind them to stay on their toes." He chuckled and speared some chicken on his fork. "Wolken is a lovely place, very little crime, but with our heads so far in the clouds some of us think a little too highly of ourselves."

Was Alowen imagining it, or did he just wink at her again? She decided to test her theory.

"I certainly see what you mean about your head being in the clouds. Are all Sky People practically giants?" There was a sharp gasp from her mother's corner that Frazyk's bellowing laughter nearly drowned out. Alowen's stomach dropped. When she looked up again, face red, her mother had composed herself, although Alowen was sure to hear about it later.

"Well, Alowen, Rogan told me you were a feisty one. It takes spunk and quite a bit of courage to manage yourself at the Element Party." The mayor dabbed his lips with a napkin, but his eyes were on hers. "I have read some of your writing. Now that I see the spirit behind it, I must say I think you will be perfect. Congratulations. Pack your bag after dinner. You will come to Wolken for your training. We have a week." Silence fell heavy on the room like a cold, wet blanket as Frazyk happily cut into his chicken. "This is amazing! I have never tasted gravy like this!"

"Old family recipe…"

Alowen's stomach gave another lurch as she saw her mother's face. She looked as if someone had knocked her out of her chair. As much as she wanted this, she hadn't planned to leave her strong, reliable mother like this. She could see her mother's eyes well up slightly as she turned away to clear the table. *What good mother would allow her children to go to Bachha?* Those Fire People lived fast and left a trail of ashes behind. Over the years, Alowen had heard it all. She could see the battle raging and rolling in her mother's head, but she tried to provide comfort with her eyes as much as possible. It's not like she would be leaving forever, and this was a huge opportunity…

In the end, her mother looked down at the table and let out a breath silently. "You can take the good luggage with you, Alowen."

"Righ' 'ish 'etlled 'en." Frazyk beamed through a large chunk of dinner roll.

"Thank you, Mom." Alowen tried to catch her own breath, which she didn't know she was holding.

She knew it was hard for her mother to let her go somewhere so far away where she couldn't protect her. *I'll make it up to you, Mom. I won't leave forever; I promise.* She would tell her a hundred times before she left. Her uncle was conspicuously silent but when she glanced at him, she thought she saw a tear spilling from his eye. He saw her looking and made a show of choking on a piece of food as an excuse to wipe his face. Luckily, the chicken dinner was delicious enough to distract from the silence at the table.

Frazyk seemed blissfully unaware that the other people in the room grappled with the heavy emotion. "You know, they don't make food like this in Wolken. It must be all these fresh vegetables. We get most of our produce from Arbor, but that isn't really the same as bringing it right inside fresh and cooking it."

Alowen was grateful when the time came to clear the plates.

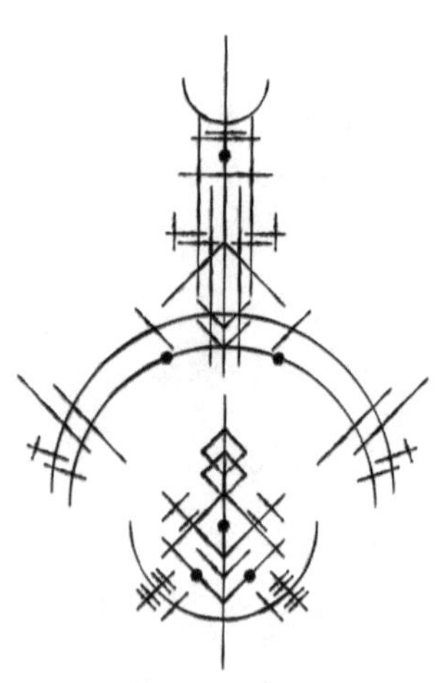

Through the wall, Alowen could hear the fire crackling as it settled into its red glow amidst muffled conversation between the adults in the other room. Around her was the familiar peace of her bedroom, wallpapered with dark green and tiny plum-colored flowers. Every time she slept, she imagined herself curled in a deep forest, the only person for miles. Her desk stood stolidly to one corner, stacked with high school journals and flyers of old stories.

Her father had built the desk even before she was tall enough for it.

The softness of it all had lulled her disbelief while she carefully gathered her favorite things together in a small pile. A few books, a hairbrush, some toiletries rolled up in a towel, a tiny velvet bag with some simple pearl studs from her mom for her sixteenth birthday. Her hands moved around woodenly. She had wanted this for so long…

Still, her hand shook slightly as she reached toward a small, stuffed sheep lying cozily on her pillow and tenderly touched the fluff on its cheek as if it would suddenly wake. Everything came up then – Frazyk's eccentric arrival, his unexpected proposal, Bachha and the Elemental Party, so many arguments with her mother over daydreaming, the surprised gratitude when her mother let her go. It was too much.

She shook with a violent sob. She could not bring "Uffy" the sheep with her. When her father had presented her with "Fluffy the Sheep," all her two-year-old vocabulary could produce was "Uffy," and it stuck. She would have to leave behind these things that gave away any childishness. She would have to banter and masquerade with the rest of the world.

She smashed Uffy into her chest as if she could press him inside her heart. She pulled back her hair and held him aloft in the moonlight. His eyes had always seemed to shine. Maybe a part of her father had left itself behind in them. Slowly, she put him down and looked around her small, moonlit bedroom trying to hold onto the details like the last strands of a dream. There were her favorite books. She couldn't pick one or two to take with her, so in the end she was probably better off leaving them all home. The same went for her Wombat, Pocket Change, and Mahogany Hats records. Those bands and their music had literally been with her all throughout high school. There was no way she could pick. She even reluctantly left behind her firestarter, something the Arbor council issued to everyone when they came of age. Old, traditional survival basic. Well, she wouldn't be needing it abroad.

Where would fate take her from here? Before she could change her mind, she hastily stuffed everything into the suitcase. She grabbed a bottle of lilac water from her desk – Mikal had given it to her as a birthday gift. Mikal... she wondered for a moment how he would react, then scoffed as the whole scene played out in her mind. He would huff about and pretend not to care, then more than likely he would find another girl to marry within a month.

She set down the bottle. It was all for the better; they would never be right for each other. She hadn't the courage to look around again, so she walked straight through her bedroom door and shut it.

The living room was cozy and warm, though the fire had burnt lower than she expected. Her mother was half asleep in a chair next to Uncle Rogan, who dreamily swirled the contents of his cup and gazed into the burning embers. On his other side, the mayor snored loudly. Half his long body was slumped over the back of his chair. He was really much too tall for any of the furniture in the house. Uncle Rogan brought his finger to his lips when he saw Alowen. They both understood they would never make it through the door if there was a proper goodbye.

He finished his drink and tapped the mass of crumpled Frazyk. Frazyk gave a little start and then a sleepy smile as he saw Alowen standing in front of him, suitcase in hand. He seemed instantly aware of the plot to keep her mother asleep.

Alowen placed her suitcase lightly on the floor and looked at her mother guiltily. She wished she had written a note to explain. But if she sat down to write, she would be at her desk all night. Still, if only she could hug her one last time…*I'll come back to you, Mom,* she promised silently. At least she had told her that about a hundred times earlier after dinner. Her mother had been wet-eyed almost all evening, but the tears would really flow tomorrow. Her own eyes welled again. She never told her mother enough how much she appreciated her.

Alowen's mother was the kind of woman who often worked too hard every day to fuss with her appearance but was always lovely. Her face practically glowed with fire from within when she smiled, and that, along with her flour-dusted apron with candies in her pockets, brought almost every child from nearby. They were drawn to her like animals to the deep shelter of the forest. They hid their faces in her arms when they had petty issues, when they had bad days, or when the woods seemed extra scary. There was no better place to cry than in her arms.

Uncle Rogan gave her a nod, and Alowen heaved a sigh. Carefully, she leaned over, and ever so slightly shifted some of her mother's auburn hair from her cheek. Alowen wouldn't see the ever-so-familiar hair for a while. She gently kissed her mother's cheek. She couldn't look into her mother's tearful eyes and walk away. But at least she could leave her that.

Then it was time. Alowen quickly embraced Uncle Rogan and gave him a look that hopefully showed him her eternal gratitude. For…for everything. Being there after her father passed away. For constantly helping her mother and her over the years. For bringing Frazyk. For staying back now and watching over home.

His gaze assured her he would handle her mother in the morning.

All matters settled, Frazyk beckoned her to come with a long, spindly finger. It took all of Alowan's willpower to keep from planting her feet to the ground, but she managed to take the necessary steps out of the door. The blast of night air on her face renewed her. She was ready for this.

On second thought… she had certainly not considered how they would be getting to Wolken.

"Don't worry, the great minds of the Sky People are always flying ahead. I brought the double saddle." Frazyk gave her what was probably his version of a reassuring smile.

"It's like you read my mind," she joked, trying to diffuse her nerves. "Are you sure your mindshield bracelet is on?"

Frazyk held up his wrist. "Not to worry, young miss. I can only know what you're thinking if you touch the bracelet and agree to let me in." He waved at Tyrq. "Shall we?"

She looked apprehensively over at Tyrq. The eagle had his eyes closed, but as they came closer he opened them, yellow and unblinking. Up close, he had at least a good two feet on Alowen. Even Frazyk barely came to his head. His beak was curved, perfect for tearing flesh. Frazyk saw her gulp and smiled again. He stroked the great bird's head and Tyrq turned his stare from Alowen. Whew. Arbor folk could link with animals' minds by remaining calm and looking them in the eyes. But there was no way she could do that with Tyrq. At least, not anytime soon.

"Um, well I've never, uh, I mean I have never really traveled on anything other than a horse."

Alowen found her knees a little weak as she imagined flying all the way to the heights of Wolken. The entire city was built on the peak of a mountain. It looked very beautiful from pictures, but she had never considered how people actually got there.

"Nothing to worry about, my lovely companion. Tyrq is a very skilled flier. You will be perfectly safe. Let me give you a hand." She took his hand hesitantly, and he pulled her onto the bird. It wasn't so terribly different than sitting on a horse. In fact, the feathers seemed to provide quite a bit of cushion beneath the saddle. There were even stirrups to secure her feet, and some sort of handlebar curving up from the saddle to hold on to. "Here's a tip!" Frazyk tied the luggage tight behind her. "If you bend a little and let the wind flow over your back, you'll keep yourself a bit more secure." He tapped the luggage as though he was pleased with his work and climbed aboard behind it. "Away we go! Hold on!"

Tyrq's great wings rose and beat the air, lifting them in a burst of wind. Alowen clenched her teeth to hold back a scream, her stomach lurching as her cottage became smaller and smaller beneath them. Every muscle in her body tightened and she gripped the handlebar until her nails bit into her skin. Trying desperately to hold on, she caught her breath against the wind as they rose higher. She fought a wave of nausea and tried not to consider what would happen if she fell off.

Eventually, she dared to open her eyes, and just like that, her fear was gone, as if the wind had plucked it away. The Arbor fanned out below her, meadows of lovely green illuminated by the full moon. Here and there, she could see flocks of sheep and herds of cows asleep in their fields. She always loved to visit their farms on sunny days. There were the old quarries glinting in the moonlight, and somewhere down there were the caves she used to explore with other children. Oh, the fun she had then, and the love she had for this place.

Other children…

Alowen jolted back to the here and now. Those days were gone. The Arbor would always be her home, but this was her true beginning. Soon she would be testing her own wings for the first time.

***

She knew they were nearing the shore as the terrain began to change. Arbor people rarely travel to the ocean, they prefer the shelter of the forest. Her father had taken her to the beach when she was very small, but she hardly remembered. The white expanse of sand was mesmerizing, the waves glittering as they danced. The water looked almost black. What was it like for the people living in the depths? Alowen had never met a water person. Apparently, they were the most ancient of all the Elements and believed to be the true guardians of the Element. That must be why their city of Allurus was off limits to the other Elements, why they rarely came out, and no one ever went in. No one really minded though. The Water People had a reputation for being fiercely protective of their own kind, even only marrying amongst themselves.

Alowen shook her head, feeling lucky. If she had been born into water, she would not be allowed to explore and travel. Uncle Rogan said punishment for any attempt at escape was excommunication, occasionally even death.

A mighty updraft swept up beneath them, and the ground pulled at her stomach again as Tyrq rose higher. The air felt colder here, the wind harsher. If the eagle's feathers weren't so warm, Alowen had no doubt she would be an ice slab. In the distance, she could see mountains jutting through grey clouds. Her heartbeat quickened. What was the training like? Would the other scribes be there or was this something Frazyk had set up specially for her? The Element Party was only a week away. That wasn't much time. How would she have the sophistication to interact with so many influential people? Clearly, Frazyk must have seen something in her, he had so much influence and experience. If he trusted she could do this, she had to learn to trust herself as well. She let loose a breath, and it came out in a thick mist. It really *was* getting colder here.

Wolken was still off in the distance, but she could see its silhouette as it reflected the moonlight. So, the stories were true. Made of white marble, the entire city rose from the top of the mountain like a stalagmite of ice. It was breathtaking. A complex pattern of spirals that occasionally burst into large globes she could only presume were buildings. Alowen couldn't imagine how such a delicate structure was made or how its many fragile limbs reached so high and remained attached. The whole thing looked like it would blow away in the strong mountain gusts.

Still, Wolken had made it this far, she told herself nervously.

As they flew in closer, the walls at the base loomed, broad, and stern. Tyrq flapped his wings a few times and soon they soared higher over the walls. It was evening but the streets were still bustling with people, most of them draped in shimmering cloaks. The city glimmered through hundreds of small windows as if the stars in the sky were lighting their homes. The beauty was eerie. Alowen felt as if they had landed on another planet.

A tower, taller than the rest, stood in the center of Wolken. Tyrq swooped up toward its peak where a large, round globe rested, covered with silver frost. This must be Frazyk's home. Well, she would definitely have to adjust to the height. Luckily, to the left of the globe rested a small landing pad where she would be able to walk inside without fainting if she could manage to not look down. Tyrq landed gracefully and bowed low to let his passengers off. Alowen's legs wobbled when her feet touched the pad, but somehow she kept herself upright.

"So, what do you think? This is Wolken!" Frazyk spread his arms proudly.

In the glow of several white lamps around them, the mayor had quite the astonishing wingspan.

"It's the most beautiful thing I have ever seen," she said through chattering teeth.

"How silly of me!! We must get you inside. You are freezing! Come."

He ushered her along a sidewalk that felt much too thin. If she lost her balance, she would go plummeting hundreds of feet to the city floor. The Sky People were obviously not afraid of heights.

The door was made out of some type of pearly glass. Just like the structure around them, it was a large circle. Frazyk put his palm flat in the center and it slid open, releasing warm air over them. Even shivering and tired, Alowen couldn't help but stare. There were rumors the Sky People, like the Water People, could control things with their minds.

Apparently, the rumors were true to some extent.

"Home sweet home!" Frazyk spun with his arms out like a delighted child.

The house was much bigger inside than it looked. Everything shimmered pale as if all the color had been covered in a sheet of frost. Some type of white fur rug lay in the center of the room sprawled out beside a fireplace that glowed strangely pink. It made the room very cozy.

"Oh, we get our fire from the Fire People." Frazyk must have seen her eyeing the fireplace.

Ah, of course. Fire from a fire person had qualities of color beyond the regular orangey-yellow. Even the temperature could rise to unimaginable levels.

Alowen kept turning in her spot. The ceiling went all the way up to a small skylight perfectly cut for a view of the moon. Spiraling ledges around the wall held small "rooms" with beds and desks. They didn't afford much privacy, but it all looked so elegant.

Frazyk hovered nearby, hands tucked behind his back. "Don't worry. I know everything seems very open, but when you close the room off you really can't see a thing."

"Close the room off?" She didn't see any walls or even a curtain, but nothing much surprised her about this place. It was all so alien.

Frazyk tutted, "Hmph, sometimes I forget you haven't traveled much. The cloud crystal that covers the door. When you are ready for your privacy, just touch the wall key, and it will close around you." Alowen frowned, perplexed, and he leaned in secretively. "Cloud crystal is our most prized product here in Wolken. It is our work, just as your farms are yours. We weave the clouds into sheets and bake them in fire. Well, not just any fire. Here, I will show you." Frazyk opened the door and stepped outside. When he came back, he had what looked like a large, wispy chunk of cotton in his hand. "This won't be quite the same because I don't have a weaving loom, but you can see how it crystallizes." He stuck his hand into the fire, cloud and all.

"Oh!!" Alowen gasped. The man had lost his mind.

He spun around laughing with a beautiful cloud sculpture in his hand, untouched by the fire.

"Wow, kid. You have more to learn than I thought. When a fire person lends you their fire, it won't burn you. Let's just say it has an intelligence of its own."

Frazyk threw her another playful wink, but her mind was exhausted from so much stimulation. She could only muster half a smile back. He put down his cloud sculpture and dusted his hands dramatically. "Where are my manners tonight? I swear. Let's get you straight to bed. You have a long day tomorrow. Let me show you to your room."

Too tired to ask what her long day would entail, Alowen trudged behind him, spiraling through the levels of his strange, luminous house. Near the top, they came to her room. This one had a fire too, though it flickered the usual orange. The bed looked heavenly, plush with fat pillows and a thick comforter. She couldn't wait to sink into it.

Frazyk pointed to a small shimmering stone on the wall next to her bed. "If you need anything, just touch this key on the wall and speak. It goes straight to my room."

"Thank you, really, for everything. With all the commotion tonight, I don't think I had a chance…" She struggled for words, but Frazyk cut her off.

"Don't mention it, kid. Just do me a favor and get some rest so you don't make a fool of us both tomorrow. We have some important meetings." Another wink, another sardonic smile. "Good night, I will close the room up for you." He placed his hand on a handprint on the wall, and it glowed pale blue. A pearly wall began to close around her room. "Enjoy!"

Alowen crawled into bed. As she had suspected, the bed was incredible. She wouldn't be surprised if it was actually made of clouds.

There would be enough time to inspect her room's strange features and adornments and process the day. Right now, she was just too tired. She cursed herself when she realized she didn't put out the fire first. Before she could get out of bed, it changed to a deep purple. It was perfect for sleeping, especially in a new room. No one but her mother knew she was afraid of the dark. She was grateful for the violet haze keeping her company.

This would all take some getting used to, but she couldn't say she minded.

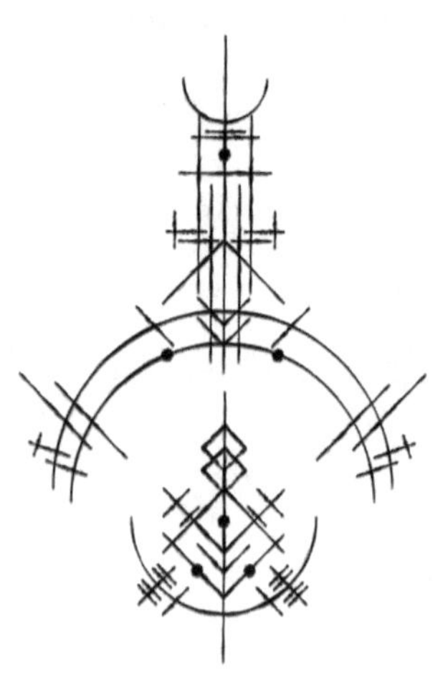

Alowen had been wrong about the skylight being there only to let the moon in. The sun fit just as perfectly in the space. It was far too early to be awake, but then again, any time would have been too early. She wished she could take this bed everywhere she went for the rest of her life. Reluctantly, she opened one eye and peered around. The room was even more incredible in the sunlight. Every surface reflected the light like ice. But it was pleasantly warm as she placed her feet on the ground. She stretched and peered out the window. The air traffic was already heavy. Mounted eagles flew among curious, shimmering bubbles that appeared completely opaque, zooming even faster than the eagles.

Alowen turned back to her room. Wow. The Arbor had nothing like that, whatever those were. Frazyk was right; she knew little about the world. She had no idea how to dress this morning for her training. What does Frazyk even mean by training? As far as she knew, the scribes of the Element Party were chosen based on their current capabilities. Ah… she may as well look as presentable as possible, at least. She walked over to her luggage and opened it, leafing through her things until she found a forest green dress. It could never hurt to dress your best. Her mother always frowned upon those types of thoughts, but then her ambition had never stretched past being a mother and wife in the Arbor.

As Alowen slipped into her dress, she recalled yesterday's events and hoped her mother was not angry with her for leaving without a proper goodbye. In her heart, she knew her mother would understand. She glanced around the room for a mirror. The walls themselves almost gave a full reflection back, but better than that, there was a small vanity in the corner.

Once she decided she looked well enough for the day's events, she walked apprehensively to the "wall key." Slowly she placed her hand in the center of the pale blue outline and smiled as the walls peeled themselves away. It took her a while to get down to the kitchen, but at least the hallway was a continuous spiral downward.

"Well, well! Good morning, my lovely house guest!"

Strange smells came from the kitchen, and she saw several pots simmering. Frazyk stirred something but flashed her a wide grin. It was odd to see him somewhat disheveled, his hair in spiky chunks pointing in all directions. He had on pajamas in a silly cloud print, his strong angular features were lovely, and his skin had a soft shimmer to it in the morning light. Even though his nose and cheek bones were delicate, his large eyes and stark eyebrows made his face striking and unusual. She gave a hesitant smile. What to make of this?

"Hungry? There is tea on the table. I must admit, I don't cook as well as your mother but still, Wolken specialty, biscuits with warm cloud berry sauce."

Alowen picked one up from a bowl beside Frazyk. It was the size of a grape from back home, but when she rolled it between her thumb and forefinger, pale green juice, almost white, oozed out, smelling like an odd mixture of grapes and blueberries. Frazyk began spooning some kind of mixture over the top of a biscuit, the same color as the berry juice.

Stranger than the food was the fact that Frazyk actually

cooked! But she definitely wasn't going to complain.

"Thank you so much for breakfast, I'm starving! I have never slept so well in all my life. Sky People are so lucky to have such heavenly beds." She carefully placed herself in the seat he had pulled back and reached for her cup of tea. Frazyk chuckled and took the seat across from her. "This is delicious, do these berries grow here?"

The Arbor famously provided produce to the rest of the Elements. But these berries were unlike anything she had ever tasted. Perhaps that was it, these berries and experiences were entirely new. Exciting beyond belief.

"Yes, these berries only grow here beside the clouds." He looked closely at the berry on his fork as if interrogating it. "I've always felt they were mocking us from the most dangerous mountain peaks." He ate the berry, delivering its fate.

She smiled to herself. She was the luckiest girl in all the Elements to be eating cloud berries at the mayor of Wolken's breakfast table of all places.

"Today I am going to introduce you to some pretty important people in the sky council before the morning meeting." He leaned in closer, "At least, they think they are pretty important." He gave her another wink.

As little as she knew Frazyk, she was becoming quite fond of him. In many ways, he reminded her of Uncle Rogan, humble with an effortless sense of humor that seemed to carry him through every situation.

"The secret in dealing with people is…" He smirked. "Well, first you must swear to carry this with you to the grave; it is confidential information." She wondered if his face hurt; he never stopped smiling.

"I swear." It was the least she could do.

"Well, the secret is, you can say anything, anything at all. Tell the truth, talk about controversial subjects, insult their mother if you wish, but do it with a smile." He tapped the corners of his own smiling mouth. "A smile is all you need in this world. If it is sincere, it will keep you out of trouble." She certainly couldn't accuse him of not testing out his theory.

To her, a smile was a spontaneous act, like a kiss. She always had a hard time forcing an expression unless it was one of confidence. She never had difficulty pretending she understood something she did not. Maybe Frazyk had something. She had better learn to practice smiling on command.

When they had finished, Frazyk dabbed his lips and stood. "The council meeting will be tedious, I warn you, but with you on your way to being a scribe you will listen in." He shrugged and gave her a what-to-do smile. "I expect you on your very best behavior."

Alowen gave a mock salute and he chuckled. Frazyk went into his room to emerge wearing a black robe that hung to the ground above his glossy, deep plum loafers. She had seen pictures of council members wearing the same robes.

After they cleaned up, they stepped back out onto the sidewalk – still far too thin – where they had landed the night before. The city looked quite different in the light, but certainly not less beautiful. It was also quite busy. Even from Frazyk's towering home, she could see people walking briskly across roads. No one seemed interested to take things slow. Also, they were in fact all nearly six-foot, some well over. In the Arbor, she was among the tallest girls, but here in Wolken, she would probably just be cutting average at best.

"Tyrq!" Frazyk let out a low whistle and the bird swooped down to perch beside his master. His bronze feathers glinted in the sun. Frazyk walked to a bucket beside the door, throwing a bloody flank of meat to the bird. "He does most of his own hunting, but you can never be sure. Slim pickings up here." Tyrq seemed satisfied and bowed its head. "Help me saddle him. You may have to do this on your own someday. Here, take this and loop it around."

Alowen took the leather strap from Frazyk's hand and awkwardly pulled it across the eagle's midsection. Tyrq's broad chest was thickly muscled, and tightening the strap felt like squeezing a tree trunk as hard as she could.

She paused. Maybe if she dared… she could… link with Tyrq? She stepped back and tried to look the eagle in the eye, but after a few seconds, she had to look down. His gaze was too intense. What in the four elements was wrong with her? Why couldn't she do it? So many of her friends could easily link with hawks and dogs when they were younger.

Frazyk didn't seem to notice what she was trying to do. "There, now bring it back over and buckle it. Make sure you pull it tight. You don't want this slipping off mid-flight."

She was shaking from the exertion, but she managed to pull the strap through the metal buckle and fasten it tightly. She double-checked it was tight enough, shuddering to think what would happen if it slipped. She noticed one of the stirrups was partially unbuckled and rushed to resolve it. She had done this so many times with horses in the Arbor but even though it was second nature, the shape of Tyrq's body was foreign to her and the saddle sat at a seventy-five-degree angle because his posture slanted rather than lay flat like a horse's back. Tyrq glanced at her briefly, his expression and eyes reminding her of a cat. The sensation made her hairs on her arms stand. Although the entire process took less than five minutes, the pressure to do it correctly made it feel like twenty.

"Perfect. The hardest part for you will be getting on. You are small for a rider. Here, I'll give you a leg up." The words made her feel like a pro. Then she got back in the saddle. The eagle lurched forward, and Alowen quickly changed her mind. Frazyk chuckled as a couple of colorful bubbles floated by. "An electric orb would be more comfortable, but you can't come to Wolken and not learn how to ride an eagle. You'll get used to it."

Alowen gritted her teeth against the wind and her flopping stomach. They swooped down to the bottom level of the city and pulled up to the side of a large building. It looked official, all gleaming chrome and ornate stonework. Maybe this was where the sky council met? There were large steps carved all the way up the marble. Everyone ascending them wore a silver robe. Frazyk scratched his eagle behind the head, curling spindly fingers under the ruff of soft feathers. "Remember, a smile is all you need in this world."

This time she didn't need to see the wink to know it was there. Frazyk had probably caused his fair share of trouble in his day. They dismounted the eagle, and Frazyk gave Tyrq several signals. He soared back up like a child after the school bell.

"Come, my dear. Time is money."

She hurried along behind his long strides. Strangely, Alowen did not feel intimidated walking on the marble steps. Maybe she was still in shock from the newness of it all. The people around her all had important expressions on their faces like they had spent years making decisions that affected the lives around them.

"Fine morning, Frazyk."

A voice startled Alowen from her daydream. She turned to see an old man with snow-white hair and a sour expression glaring at them. But Frazyk didn't seem bothered.

"Sure is, Sarth. Meet my new partner in crime. This is Alowen. She is Rogan's niece, the one I was telling you about."

The old man's face softened. "You are a lucky young woman, Alowen. Many people long for the experience of being a scribe. You know, I was a scribe when I was your age. I never regretted it, not for one second. Good luck, my dear. Frazyk, don't you dare corrupt any more of our youth! Don't listen to a word he says, young lady." He shuffled along up the steps.

She stood on her tiptoes and whispered to Frazyk. "He sure looks like he regrets more than he is letting on." He whirled around with a surprised laugh.

"Such snark! I have truly underestimated you, young lady!" He leaned in close to avoid the ears of passersby. "I can't say for sure, but there is a rumor he met the love of his life at the Element Party. She was from Bachha, both her parents Fire People. His parents are purists, both twelfth-generation air, so he never married. Never stopped thinking about her." He frowned as they kept walking. "Apparently, she disappeared into Allurus a year after he refused to marry her. No one really knows what happened."

For a moment, he looked confused and forlorn. The steps seemed to clear off as they reached the top. Towering, paneled glass doors separated the busy city from the pristine, calm council world inside.

Inside the large building was a cavernous auditorium where an assembly was taking their seats. High above them were incredible pearly statues carved into the ceilings. There were battle scenes with horses and people from the Arbor, ornate party scenes in Bachha, and quiet nature scenes of the Wolken mountains.

"You stay with me, my dear. High council conducts these meetings. I will be giving the updates at the end." She was relieved to see Frazyk's smirk return. "We have the best seats in the house."

He ushered her up to the front of the room to sit. He was right, they could see almost all the faces in the room. The council sat at the very front in gold robes, looking elderly and austere. A man with metallic glasses approached the podium with a black book. He opened it and looked around.

"We are now in session, please be seated. I am Cornelius Watson, your council secretary. First on the agenda is presented by Simona on the cloud berry pickers union."

The man stepped away, and a blonde woman approached the podium holding a large bundle of papers.

"Good morning. The Cloud Berry Picker's Union is requesting additional weeks off due to the stressful and dangerous nature of climbing on the cliffs of the mountains to obtain the berries. They are requesting three additional weeks built into their contract with pay remaining as is. For hundreds of years, cloud berry pickers did what they must to feed their families, but almost eleven percent of cloud berry pickers die by falling every year. With the snows getting thicker and lasting longer, that number has risen..."

The issue of worker's rights was something close to Alowen's heart. She grew up hearing her mom and Uncle Rogan talk about it. She listened raptly as someone stood to respond to the woman. It seemed only right for people risking their lives for something as silly as a berry. Yes, cloud berries were part of the culture, but no one would die if they disappeared, and still every year she heard about harvester deaths.

Over an hour later, Alowen could hardly listen to another word. Her mind was all over the universe, anywhere but in this room. Even though she was fast becoming a part of the world of adults, some of their business still seemed overdone. Was all of this debating really necessary? Wasn't there a more efficient way of dealing with matters? When there was a truly important event for her school, voting seemed to settle most questions, but she guessed there were more complications as issues became more important. She often heard Uncle Rogan talking about the corruption of the council and how it needed to be closely watched. Apparently, when her father was her age, he was part of a party of rebels who overthrew a faction of the Arbor council trying to raise the taxes for the local farmers. He became a hero in his own right, the "no farmer's tax" law had not budged since he and his counterparts put it in place. One thing was for certain, the world outside the Arbor was even more complicated.

Before she knew it, Frazyk was tapping her wrist, clearing his throat quietly. "Alowen, try to look awake. I will be back to fetch you for something much more exciting in just a minute. I conduct the end of the meeting." He exaggerated a wince. "Regretfully, it is just as sleep-inducing as the last hour has been."

She smiled. It was refreshing to meet an adult who understood the tediousness of certain adult rituals.

"Two last matters of business. I want to remind everyone. Last week Vino Masso submitted a form with a hundred and fifty signatures petitioning the sky council to raise the wage for mixed Element employees. We will be voting by the end of the week, so a friendly reminder." Frazyk paused, but there was silence. He sighed. "Just so we all still remember, Vino Masso is the President of the Element Laison Federation."

Alowen raised her eyebrows. What was the Element Liaison Federation, and why was everyone so quiet now? She would have to ask Frazyk more later.

Frazyk shook his head. "Right. Next, we have complaints that traffic is leaving, ahem, droppings tracked upon the streets. There have even been incidents of direct contact with clothing. Proposals for reparations will be submitted in written format. We have arranged for a portion of the budget to cover potty training for eagles." Alowen stifled a laugh. Fascinating as it was watching Frazyk fake seriousness, she had more important thoughts at hand. Frazyk mentioned that whatever was coming was more exciting than her current circumstances. She wondered if Tyrq still soared around happily. It hadn't even been a full day yet and already she felt like a whole new person. Her ears brought her back to Frazyk's voice. "And that adjourns our fifty-ninth annual meeting."

The assembly took their time getting up and dispersing, but Frazyk marched for the door. Thankfully, Alowen was ready. She kept on his heels.

"Fifty-ninth?" Alowen whispered as they walked out of the building.

Some building staff and pedestrians greeted their mayor and gave Alowen curious looks. She practiced her new forced smile. People seemed to respond well, at least they smiled back.

"I know, it's absolutely horrible, but I get to live in the silver house at the top of Wolken!" He sniggered, and she wondered if he wasn't a twelve-year-old boy masquerading as an adult. "So now we get to have some real fun. You are really going to like this. Have you heard of Wombat?" For the second time in as many days, the color drained from Alowen's face. Wombat? One of the most famous bands in all of the Elements?

"Uh, yeah, sure. I know who they are. I have a lot of friends who listen to their music."

Alowen really hated looking like she was impressed by fame. The problem was she was more than impressed by it, she was downright envious. The thought of being paid to do something she adored and having people compliment her for it made her crazy. Anyone who said they didn't want this was lying through their teeth.

"Right." Something about Frazyk's expression told her he saw right through her. "Well, your luck is in today. Turns out they are passing through, so I managed to grab lunch with them today at Sielo. They are all great guys. Let me know if your friends ever want tickets to a show."

Alowen struggled to maintain the appearance that her body was not melting from the inside out all over the alabaster sidewalk. Lunch. With Wombat. At Sielo. It was one of the most expensive restaurants in all of the Element. The band was certainly not the only famous attraction there.

Her feet felt heavy along the pale, beautiful street. She wanted to pinch herself, but she couldn't give away her excitement. She may have a sneaking suspicion that Frazyk understood parts of her she didn't want to admit, but she wasn't ready to blow her cover.

"Don't worry, we have an hour so you can change into something more formal."

Alowen's stomach flopped. She had absolutely nothing to wear to a place like Sielo. This green dress was too shabby to meet Wombat in! She had brought some money to shop but an hour certainly wasn't long enough. Does her skin look grey? She tried to stifle her nervousness, but her heart pattered like hailstones on a roof. It was so overwhelming here. Arbor people were so unassuming, they rarely even wore shoes. Now she was expected to have a casual lunch with some of the biggest celebrities in the Element?

Suddenly Frazyk burst out laughing again, in his charming habit. "Really child, if you don't take life less seriously you will spontaneously combust. Do you really think your uncle and I would spring something like this without having you covered?" She gazed up at him in surprise and he winked back, gesturing at the sky without looking. "There is a brand-new dress complete with proper jewelry waiting back at the house, gorgeous blue and all. Your uncle made sure you had a formal wardrobe ready. He knew there would be enough stress with the Element Party only a week away. We hired a personal shopper and gave her your measurements."

Alowen let out a breath she was unaware she had been holding. When she opened her mouth to speak, a nervous giggle slipped out. Just then a shadow passed over them before wheeling back. Tyrq landed gracefully beside them and fixed his yellow eyes on Alowen, but this time she was too relieved to dread an eagle's stare. Her world was at peace.

"Not another word, child! Up you go," Frazyk swooped her effortlessly onto Tyrq's back, and she went through the motions, tucking her feet into the stirrups.

Tyrq flapped his wings in a couple of beats, and there was the familiar tugging sensation on Alowen's belly. She leaned in and closed her eyes as the late morning breeze caressed her face. She let her mind go blank to the familiar sound of feathers rustling and the gentle feeling of her body lifting to the sky.

Alowen blinked to cold gusts whipping around her face. The daydream felt so real for a minute as if HER pillows were piled cozily around her and Uffy was tucked against her chest. From outside her bedroom, she had even smelled her mother's mouthwatering Sunday roast. The thought of her mother left an aching pit inside her stomach. She should write her mother a letter as soon as she had a bit of time to herself—whenever that might be.

Tyrq turned a corner, and Frazyk's slim tower home came into view. She gripped the handlebars in front of her and bent herself over the great bird's head as winds flung her hair back. What would her mother think to see her soaring amongst the clouds like this?

"Very good!" Frazyk called behind her. "You are learning!"

They arced high over the sphere on top of the tower, and Tyrq landed back on the all-too-thin sidewalk, crouching low.

"I won't spoil any surprises," Frazyk said as they climbed off. "I am no fashion expert, but I bet you will be the envy of many young girls in the dress our personal shopper picked out. If you like her work, I will introduce you, and the two of you can work out an arrangement for future engagements."

Envy of many young girls? Dress? Personal shop—

Suddenly Wombat sprang back into her mind! She had less than an hour before lunch! Dressdressdress! If this personal shopper got her anything decent, at the very least, she would owe her forever! She scuffled alongside Frazyk as he placed his palm atop the mysterious blue handprint on the door, which moved aside with a small hiss.

"It should all be laid out for you on the bed in your room. I had the housekeeper come and set everything up while we were gone. I would check your dresser too if I were you." He winked.

"Oh, thank you! Thank you!" For a moment, Alowen forgot her manners and turned into a normal teenage girl. As usual, she caught herself and became embarrassed. "I mean, thank you. I just, um, I just really appreciate this."

Frazyk laughed, a knowing smile spreading across his face. "Don't mention it, kid." He jabbed a finger upstairs, practically hopping on the spot with excitement. "Well? Don't just stand there! We have twenty-five minutes. Go get dressed!"

Alowen sprinted to her room and placed her hand upon the door key. As the wall slid away slowly, *too slowly*, she saw what had to be the most beautiful dress she had ever owned! It was royal blue with a gorgeous turquoise lace petticoat peeking out from the bottom. The lace was definitely handmade; it was so intricate. The cut of the dress was very simple, strapless, and looked as though it would fall just below the knee. The most sparkly turquoise gem earrings sat on top of the dress. Each one, the size of a cloudberry! A small note underneath said, "Uncle Rogan with love." With a pang of guilt, she hoped they were costume jewelry and not real. Uncle Rogan really shouldn't have spent so much money. He had no children of his own and loved to spoil her.

Hurriedly, but as carefully as she could, she put on the dress and hastily looked around at the dresser where Frazyk said her gift was waiting. Sure enough, something glinted—a beautiful silver hairpin dripping with more turquoise jewels. Eyeing herself in the mirror, she put on the earrings as the finishing touch. She hardly recognized herself.

The walk down to the living room felt very long and already nerves gathered in her stomach. It's just as well she was wearing flats and not heels! She had no idea what to say to Frazyk, but he broke the tension before it could collect any momentum.

"Woooo hoo! And who might you be? My name is Frazyk. I'm the mayor of Wolken." He gave her his best love-struck look, but his signature smirk peeked out from beneath.

She elbowed him in the ribs with a mock scowl.

"Ow, ow! That's not very ladylike, you know."

"Can we please get this show on the road?"

No cure for nervousness like a good dose of sarcasm. The suspense may actually kill her.

Frazyk took the sass like a champ. "Hasty, are we? Okay, let's move." He whistled and Tyrq popped his head through the window. Frazyk waved elegantly to the door. "Shall we?"

He helped her up first and climbed on in front. By now, her feet entered the stirrups naturally and her hands took the handlebars without a second thought. Her mind slid to Wombat. How was she going to chew, let alone swallow her lunch? What would Wombat think? What are they like? Would the wind mess up her nicely pinned hair?

One of their songs from their earlier albums actually rose to mind as they took off. Jorry's lead vocals floated in with guitar notes.

> *"When you take in the sunset,*
> *Breathe out all of your regret,"*

Raydan and Stepno's backing harmonies joined.
"OoowooOooOo…
"Life is just too short to not be free,
At the edge of the world and the sea."

The lyrics from Alowen's childhood hummed through her mind, soft and crooning against the howl of wind around her. After a while, she couldn't help but relax. It's alright. The Wombat boys had produced such a comforting song, and so many others like it. They are sure to be chill people.

Right?

"Over there!" Frazyk's long arm reached past her, pointing. "Sielo, up ahead!"

Tyrq dipped lower to avoid another eagle, and as the shadow of its wings and tail passed overhead, Alowen saw it. A sparkling, slate-grey building stood proudly in front of her, a stark contrast to the glimmering white buildings surrounding it. It looked sleeker and more modern. Even other eagle riders couldn't pass it without at least glancing its way, Sielo was just that magnetic. Her heart pounded again. Soon…Wombat…

Tyrq began a smooth descent. On closer inspection, the walls were open and draped in billowy cream linens that caught the wind like a sail. Eagles perched patiently on a cloud-like sculpture to the side of the building. Beside it, a patio filled with waiters and diners extended outward. When they landed, the entire thing bobbed a little but held. Panic tightened Alowen's grip on the handlebars for a moment, but Frazyk chuckled behind her.

"It's safe, I promise. The air magic that helped build this cloud crystal platform is a self-levitation charm of sorts that keeps it afloat. If it reaches its limit, I think it produces some bubble that keeps new guests from landing. Luckily, I made reservations, so they kept us a spot!"

He gracefully dismounted and reached to help her down. Her sandal caught in the stirrup, and she stumbled a bit. Frazyk gave her another one of his "reassuring" smiles, but she was too busy pretending not to be embarrassed to notice. Luckily, the people on the patios were far too important to notice. Many of these famous faces were deeply invested in their lunchtime conversations. They were all finely dressed, each one looking as though they belonged there. Even when one or two caught sight of Frazyk, they only gave him a curt nod before focusing somewhere else. Wow, even the mayor of Wolken himself only got so much notice. Frazyk winked and then rolled his eyes at Alowen.

"The wealthy, *so* above everyone," he quipped.

"Mayor Frazyk, Sielo's greetings!" She nearly jumped. A young maître d' had come silently up to them. "This way, if you please!"

Soft music and wine glasses tinkled in the background as the maître d' led them swiftly past Sielo's many dining lounges. It was even more elegant inside. Some walls were light jade, others were jet black with gold veins. They were moving so quickly, Alowen only had time to see a waiter present a table with a crimson lobster on a bed of ice, surrounded by bright lemon slices and probably a dozen fat proudly whiskered prawns. Another one passed her holding a long, dark green bottle and its deep, strong smell made her head swim for a second. "Our best aged wines from our cellars," their maître d' explained. "The oldest is as expensive as a whole apartment."

Finally, they arrived at a private table in the back overlooking a pond as still and calm as a mirror. The maître d' seated Frazyk first and then turned to Alowen.

"Miss."

She was seated just in time to see a fish leap out of the water. It caught the sunlight and flashed like spun gold.

She gasped. "Frazyk, is there anything in Wolken that doesn't shimmer?"

"Why yes, my dear. Some of Wolken's most famous personalities are as dull as a piece of moldy straw; I assure you." He picked up a menu with the day's lunchtime specials. "I really insist you try the filet of elk. It's served with a green salad and the cream of pumpkin soup."

Fillet of elk? The people of Wolken sure do enjoy some unique cuisine!

"Wow, that sounds amazing. But back to the question. I mean, why is everything here so shimmery? I mean the people … the animals …" She stared back at the pond hoping to see more of the exotic life beneath.

"Well, my dear, that is one of life's mysteries, I suppose." Frazyk folded one long leg over another. "Maybe living so close to the light, we absorb more of its qualities. Like attracts like, you know." He lowered his voice. "I'll tell you a secret. Word has it Sielo has a mixed person working in their kitchens."

Sielo?? A mixed employee? Alowen couldn't believe her ears. The government of each Element really frowned upon mixing Elements. It did still happen occasionally. There were rumors of mixed children being born with special powers as the gifts unique to each element combined in strange ways. Mixed-Element people faced a lot of discrimination from the intense fear surrounding their existence. There was Soren, for example. A handsome, older boy from high school whose mother was from the Arbor but whose father was apparently from Allurus. The school banned him from the swim team for "having an unfair advantage." A high-class establishment like Sielo surely wouldn't even think about employing a mixed person.

She frowned. "Wouldn't they lose customers?"

"Well, there was always that risk. But from what I heard,

only the owner and the manager know who this mixed employee is. Maybe their gift somehow makes the flavors and smells stronger? Or the décor more beautiful?" Frazyk said thoughtfully. Then he shook himself. "Ah, but now I am guessing and making stuff up. All I have are what one person heard from another person who got it from two others down the line. We'll think about this another time." He glanced behind her and waved. "Boys, over here! How are you? Good to see you!"

Oh my God, it was Wombat! Sielo and this whole secret was so mesmerizing Alowen had nearly forgotten! She was certain she blushed but hopefully they didn't notice. Jorry, Raydan, and Stepno were too busy shaking hands with Frazyk and clapping him on the shoulder. They looked exactly the same in person as they did on the album covers. Well, maybe a bit taller. Like some of the Arbor's Fire People visitors, their skin was flushed pink with excitement right now. In concerts, they were even known to catch on fire a little during some of the more intense guitar riffs. She couldn't help but blink at their attire. Jory was wearing velvet pants as pink as crushed raspberries and a ripped-up black t-shirt with brightly colored images of the paper mâché "pets" that people kept in Bachha.

Raydan's trousers looked like a checkerboard of pale gray and dark purple, and he wore an oversized slate turtleneck sweater along with black sunglasses. Stepno was dressed in black from head to toe, but a jeweled skull flashed crimson from his neck, dangling by a chain of smaller crimson jewels.

Frazyk gestured to her. "Boys, this is Alowen. She is the scribe chosen this year to represent the Arbor at the Element Party."

Alowen thought she must be tomato-red by now, but she managed to look them in the face and wave.

"Righteous!" The three spilled out almost in unison. "Lovely to meet you."

Jorry took her hand and kissed it lightly. Oh, so warm!

"Right on." Raydan gave her a curious once-over and then shook her hand, his grip firm and confident.

"Can't wait to read your stuff!" Stepno added, grinning at her.

Somehow she managed to roll her eyes playfully. "There's already so much I can say."

"Just make us look good," Stepno said, and the table burst into laughter.

For one of the world's most famous bands, it was crazy to see Wombat still be a normal trio of boys. They talked about school—apparently, their parents insisted they keep up at least some classes in between tours and recording music and told crazy tour stories without sounding arrogant. Who knew they nearly fell to their deaths once when their eagles were caught in a freak storm?? When the maître d' came back with glorious dishes, they wowed over the food just like she did, even though they could probably afford to eat the same kinds of meals every day. As for her, lunch was one for the books! The fillet of elk was seared just nice on the outside but tender pink inside, and the cream of pumpkin soup was…different from what her mother made at home. Maybe not better. Maybe. Just different. But it was delicious without a doubt.

The Wombat boys were also so helpful with their stories about last year's Element Party.

"Keep an eye out for the flaming cocktail jugglers!"

"Every year, there's the man who trained his rabbit to saw *him* in pieces and then put him back!"

"This musician somehow copied the voices of dolphins and warblers in his seven-pipe flute!"

By the time lunch was over, she had their latest album in

hand with their signatures and a note that said, "Can't wait to see you at the party!" No one from home would ever believe this. If they could see her now! If everyone at this year's Party was as easy to chat with as these three, maybe this whole celebrity ordeal was going to be a cinch after all. Maybe she was getting a little full of herself, but it almost seemed like Raydan had a crush on her! He personally cut her a slice of blueberry tart and practically made her promise to come backstage after their opening night next week.

"Alowen?"

She closed her eyes.

The sky above Wolken was orange and all deep purples.

"Alowen, can you hear me?"

There was a gentle breeze wisping past her. Tyrq was gliding serenely up towards a familiar-looking tower…

"Come in Alowen … I repeat, Wolken to Alowen."

Frazyk snapped his fingers in front of her face. Oh goodness! It was evening and they were already back on the sidewalk in front of Frazyk's place.

She blinked and put her hand up to her face. "Wow, sorry, I don't know where my mind is at. I mean, well, I do but you know, this is just so …"

"Overwhelming?" Frazyk finished good-humoredly. He turned to open the door and she followed. "Yes, I know. That's why tomorrow will be nice and boring. I want to give you lots of time to sit through your tutoring and daydream about Raydan." The wink, the infamous wink.

She couldn't help but laugh.

Wait one second though… "Tutoring?" School was over, no way.

"Yes, my dear, this is not optional." Frazyk led the way into his living room and stretched his hands into the inviting fireplace. "Your writing from school is lovely, but the Element Party will be a whole other level, so we'll need to make sure you can hold your own in celebrity interviews. It is very different from a regular conversation like we had with our Wombat friends. There is an art form to gathering confidential information. Give trust to get trust. If you tell your secrets, you will hear many of theirs. The Wolken scribe has already flown to Bachha to meet some of the celebrities' agents. But don't compare yourself with her. Speaking of trust"—he turned back to her looking amused—"I have a very trusted friend coming to teach you her ways early in the morning, so shuffle on upstairs to bed. I believe the housekeeper laid out a towel and bathrobe for you if you would like a shower."

"Alright, alright."

She tried to be sullen, but it was simply impossible. Already sleepiness was setting in. She floated to her room, undressed in a haze, and stared into the purple blaze of the fire as she sprawled on her bed, the entire day swirling around her head. A shower would have to wait till morning… She barely noticed when her thoughts ended and her dreams began.

Morning came too quickly, as usual. Alowen slowly stretched and smiled in the patch of sun casting into her room. Raydan had been singing a charming melody just for her. Then her talk with Frazyk from last night floated back in. Oh no, her "tutor" was coming over. Boring! At least she could stay in comfortable clothes. She rolled off the bed, grabbed her towel, and headed to the bathroom. Mini torches set into the wall were alight with white-green fire as she stepped in, and a pleasant flowery mist coated the air. A tub was filled with steaming water where white lilies bobbed. She dipped a hand in, and the water was just warm enough, even with the steam. It looked and felt *so* inviting, she knew she was coming back at the end of the day.

Later, as she brushed her teeth, her hair in a bun, she inspected the strange bottles lined along the shelf. Unicorn milk cream for skin gel. Fairy spore powder for soothing burns. Essence of Eagle Talon, *Guaranteed to Attract the Opposite Sex*. She blinked at that.

She really doubted Frazyk needed help with this. Despite his quirkiness, he was quite handsome for a man his age. More confident than most younger men too if she had to be honest. It must be a bottle he hadn't used for a while. She threw on some jeans and a t-shirt and gave her reflection a once-over before heading out into the hallway. As she neared the kitchen, she could hear chatter. The murmurs were low but when her footsteps got closer, they stopped completely.

Alowen sighed deeply, time to meet her tutor. She moved the final few steps into the kitchen and stopped at the sight of a striking woman sitting at the breakfast table with Frazyk. Her hair was shaved into a tight buzz cut and her skin looked like glossed ebony in the light. Her cheekbones were angled handsomely sharp, and the smile she gave Alowen flashed white teeth.

Frazyk lifted his mug. He was already dressed in a sharp-fitting midnight blue suit that almost looked black in low lighting. She wondered if Wolkenians had to have their clothes specially made since they were so tall.

"Good morning, Alowen! This is Adenike, and she is going to be working with you today."

Alowen raised a hand, a little awkwardly. Sure, Wombat was one of the most popular, high-profile celebrities but it's one thing to have casual lunch with them. It just felt a little…vulnerable to have someone comment on her writing.

"I'll let her introduce herself more. But believe me, she's one of a rare bunch in the writing world." Frazyk drained his mug and put it into the sink. "I should get going. I will let you ladies get to it! There is coffee and cloud berry scones on the counter. Help yourself to anything from the fridge. I will probably be back early with dinner."

"Thank you, Frazyk. Have a good day." Adenike's voice had a hypnotic quality that relaxed the tension in Alowen's shoulders.

They watched as Frazyk mounted Tyrq and flew off. Then Adenike stood and reached out her hand. "I hear you are new in town, Alowen. How are you liking it?"

"It's…very new." Shyly, Alowen took the other woman's

hand. Adenike briefly closed her other hand over Alowen's as they shook. "Cloud crystals, a bed like a marshmallow, I think I'm starting to get the hang of riding a giant eagle, and this entire city shimmers looking so…"

"Fancy?" Adenike suggested with a slow grin.

Alowen giggled. "I was going to say lovely, but sure."

Adenike found herself relaxing. This wasn't going to be like school after all. She sat and picked up a cloud berry scone.

"Well, more about me." Adenike sat back down and took her mug again. "After I graduated from Astara Institute, I began working for Wolken's news station as a journalist. When my dear friend, Frazyk, told me what a fine writer you are and how you are our scribe for the Element Party, I just had to meet you myself. I knew you must be very special. Frazyk is very particular about who he chooses for the Element Party."

Astara! Wolken's prestigious writing school! Her hazel eyes were deep and sincere. Alowen blushed at the look and her words.

"Thank you; you are really kind."

Adenike waved it away casually. "You'll hear more and more of the same in time, I promise. I went to the Element Party when I was your age, actually, so this is experience talking." She chortled, pulling out a satchel. "Before I came over, I wondered – you are a writer, so what kind of books do you like?"

"Umm…" Alowen scratched her head, puzzled. "I do like fantasy, and adventure books, like…like…*Ballet of the Garden Swifts,* by Elema, or *The Sheep who Clothed the Lion* by Dexran. I grew up learning how to write creatively from those two authors."

In fact, she had two whole shelves back home just for them.

Adenike grinned, "Great taste! I love Elema and Dexran too! I thought Elema's *Buffalo Emperor* trilogy was her best work yet. What do you think?"

"Oh!" Alowen scratched her head. "Yes, that series was good too. I kind of wish Tallahan had gone with her human girl in the end. But I guess the wilds were best for her." She sighed. "Only Elema could write a bittersweet ending like that. But it was done so well."

"She's one of the best, right?" Adenike put a finger to her lips. "Rumor has it she's hiding somewhere writing her next book. And I actually met Dexran once, right before he became a bestseller!"

"No way!" Alowen held her hand over her mouth. "You met Dexran?!"

"He signed my copy of *The Water Dragon Legends*." Adenike pulled a thin children's book from her bag and slid it to her. The cover had a sigil that looked like the eight stages of the moon cycle.

Alowen's eyes widened. According to a legend thousands of years old, a water dragon emerged from the ocean on one new moon and covered the world in ice, killing everyone but the Allurans, and leaving them to be the oldest race. Those were the Frozen Years. Of course, the other races emerged over time and together formed the still-developing world they knew today.

When she was still a baby, Dexran had somehow gotten their permission to put this legend of theirs in print, the first – and only – outsider to get that privilege. Alowen opened the thin paperback. Sure enough, his untidy autograph was on the first page. She stared in shock.

Adenike leaned in as though she was sharing a secret. "You can borrow it while you are here. I thought it would be the perfect gift, especially if you didn't know Dexran. Lots of bookstores don't sell this anymore. Allurus only allowed ten copies printed."

Alowen almost cried. "You…are…my…favorite person now."

"There, there, wipe your tears," Adenike smiled. "Alright, you'll have to tell me what you think about it later, but for now, I want to switch to your own writing."

Alowen straightened and slid the book aside. Where was this going?

"First"—Adenike slid back her left sleeve, revealing a mind shield bracelet. This one looked thicker than the average kind—"would you be okay granting me permission into your mind? It helps me better appreciate the stories people tell. I'll only be able to know and see what we are talking about, nothing else."

Alowen hesitated for a moment. She had never let anyone into her mind, but she couldn't feel any safer around this lady.

"Okay." She reached and touched the glassy bracelet made of cloud crystal. After a while, the bracelet went from green to a milky white.

"Now, Frazyk mentioned your articles from school, and I did get a bit of time to look at two or three. But it got me curious…" Adenike carefully pulled out some school magazines from her bag, and shifted volumes aside, turning a few pages.

Alowen inhaled anxiously, but her new friend didn't notice.

"Let's see, let's see…" These were almost four years' worth of articles she had written for her school magazine, and it felt like years as Adenike patiently sifted through the small pile. Finally, she tapped one of them. "'Terriers or Turtles for Therapy?' Your first ever article, I think. I know the story, but what was that like for you?"

"Well…" Alowen set aside her half-eaten scone, making

sure she swallowed before she spoke. "Wow, I had been so little then…I was still so…nervous putting work out there, but that particular assignment was perfect for putting me at ease."

Adenike nodded slowly, listening.

"I guess I decided to do it because well, I was inspired by Noah. I know the article introduced him a bit but when I wrote it. I didn't want to tell everyone how much studies were stressing him out. But they made him so anxious. Poor kid." She met her tutor's gaze. "Two of the few things that brought him calm were his pets: Softy his box turtle and Safety his Cairn Terrier. The article did mention that, but not how he always talked about them in homeroom." A smile slowly trekked across her face. It was all coming back now. "One day, he asked the principal if they could hang out with him in the field after school for his friends to play with, and amazingly, she said 'sure.'"

Adenike looked right at her, her chin resting on her hands. "Who wouldn't say no, right?"

"Almost everyone wanted to spend time with Softy and Safety – me included – and next thing we knew, Jane our counselor thought it would be a good idea to find more Terrier and Turtle owners over the Arbor and invite them to school for a special Therapy Day." Alowen had to smile again. "I remember me and a few others helping Noah write letters to convince those people."

She could still see the circle they sat in, carefully writing each letter, and then rewriting, Softy lying peacefully next to her. "That was one of the few times I had seen the whole school look so happy. After that, the school magazine asked if I would like to go around with a poll asking who relaxed more with a terrier or a turtle, and then write a piece off that." She leaned back with a breath. "There was so little stress that came with that. Fitting, isn't it?"

"That was beautiful," Adenike said quietly. She stirred her coffee. "Thank you for sharing that with me. This is one way you can interview someone, do you see? Try asking about something that feels very comfortable, maybe something fun and memorable in their past." She pointed to the Terrier or Turtles article. "When you talk to these people, the celebrities you are going to meet, just remember they are sick to death of talking about the same old things. Money, power, and fame become so blah once you have them. They want to remember passion and joy. Ask them who their first love was. Ask them what their favorite meal as a child was. Ask them what their favorite book is and why. Listen when they answer you. Find the pieces of them in their answers and build a picture of who they really are, that way you can gracefully interview someone without crossing lines or making them feel uncomfortable."

Alowen listened in awe. This tutoring session wasn't a lecture like she had expected. Adenike gave her a space to speak and share. None of her teachers in high school had taught so personally and invitingly. She would most definitely remember this.

Adenike picked up a butter knife. "Those were some cute little terriers and turtles, seriously. I could see Softy and Safety right next to you. It's not that I can read people's minds, exactly, but when I am interacting with someone, I do see pictures, almost snapshots of their memories and what they are thinking about. Sometimes I can feel what they are feeling, too." She took a delicate bite. "That comes from having a father from Wolken and a mother from Bachha. My fire isn't as intense as a normal fire person's. I think I inherited more from my father. I think my mother's fire probably just intensified the natural Wolkenian ability to read people. Here, close the link." She offered Alowen her bracelet again.

Alowen blinked as she tapped it, and the crystal turned

back to green. "Wow, you are mixed-element? I mean there are so few mixed people these days." Suddenly, the past two days seeped back in – Frazyk talking about some petition to raise mixed Element wages, the rumor Sielo might have a secret mixed employee. She lowered her voice reflexively. "Do-do many people know?"

Adenike laughed, her teeth flashing, eyes sparkling. "No need to whisper here. It's just us. Thank you though. In my childhood, I was definitely just as nervous. Growing up in Wolken, people did know I was mixed Element, so I had many difficulties as a child. That's why it was always my dream to be a scribe, to give a voice to the struggles people face in this world."

Alowen thought back to Soren. He always seemed like such a loner. Even when she tried talking to him and be his friend, he never responded much. For a time, she had always been intrigued by him, but maybe he felt she was just another non-mixed person pitying him.

She shook off the thought. "So, you could really see pictures in my mind? Mixed folks really do have…special powers and stuff?"

"Well…" Adenike wiped her lips and brushed crumbs off her blouse. She seemed to consider her answer carefully. "Yes, Alowen. There are things about me that only mixing the elements can explain. In some ways, it has made life even more difficult for me because a lot of people in my industry feel I have an unfair advantage."

"That must be tough. Why don't you find another place to work, where people don't know you?"

Adenike shrugged, "Although I have had much success in the world, it's difficult for me to feel like I really belong anywhere. When I was your age, I thought about moving to Bachha and staying there. It's easier to blend in when you are surrounded by other misfits. The truth is, Wolken is my home, and I would rather have to work harder for the respect of my peers than run and hide in fear of being judged."

Alowen could imagine a younger Adenike spending late nights at her desk long after everyone had gone home, editing journal articles, rewriting then rewriting, practicing interviews by herself. "You must have gotten some friends at work."

"Oh, some. But there's not much time, unfortunately." Adenike poured more coffee into her cup. "The work can be so demanding. Thankfully, I love writing, you know?" She chuckled and sipped.

But surely there had to be more companionship in a job where one talked to so many people… "Have you ever become friends with anyone you interviewed? I mean, you care so deeply about them. You want to know about them not their wealth or glory."

Adenike looked off to the side of the room. There was a pause. *Oh no.* Alowen held her breath. *I have asked the wrong thing.* Finally, Adenike looked back at her.

"Yes, there was a time when I developed a very close friendship with someone I worked on a story with. It didn't end well. Mixing work with love is not something I ever recommend."

Adenike took another slow sip and Alowen fidgeted. She shouldn't have asked. Maybe if she pretended to get a glass or something behind her, they could move away from this. She turned and frowned as she noticed something. Was Adenike looking at the mantle? Frazyk's picture with the key to the city was framed there proudly. But then again, she could just be tilting her cup as she drank. Maybe it was nothing.

They were silent for a moment before Adenike seemed to regain her composure.

"Well, Alowen. I have two assignments for you. Here."

She drew out a sheaf of papers. "A list of the Elemental Party celebrity guests for this year, with a profile on each of their backgrounds and achievements, and some of their past interviews. Study up on them, and I want you to spend some time practicing interview questions in the mirror."

Ohhh no. Homework?? Alowen groaned, but Adenike shrugged apologetically.

"We have six more days. That's not much time, so I want you to take this seriously."

Alowen felt a mixture of fear and excitement. She stood and cleared away the coffee cups as Adenike packed the school magazines into her bag. "Adenike, thank you. I really appreciate you helping me. I know you must be busy, and you didn't have to—"

Adenike waved her words away with a smile. "Like I said, Alowen. Any friend of Frazyk's is a friend of mine. Anytime. I will be at the Element Party as well, so if you get stuck while we are there, don't hesitate to find me and ask." She drew Alowen into a hug and said, "I will see you in two days! Stay focused." Just like that, she headed for the door and left.

Alowen looked out the window and noticed dark clouds across the sun. She wondered what her mother was making for lunch, or if she was even cooking much now that Alowen had gone. Well, Uncle Rogan would still have to eat.

What could she do now? She flipped through the files Adenike had left her and sighed. She didn't feel like doing much reading now. Perhaps she could go for a walk and make a new friend in this city, but it looked about ready to rain, judging by the clouds, and she didn't feel like rummaging through her luggage for a coat.

Instead, she fiddled with the wall key, trying to get the strange pink fire in the fireplace to come alive as it was when she had first entered. When she placed her hand on the wall near the fire, a blueprint appeared, glowing for several seconds. Soon after, a pleasant rose-pink fire lit the room.

As thunder boomed in the distance, she grabbed a scone and turned on more water for tea. Frazyk had told her to take anything from the fridge so maybe he wasn't coming back for lunch, but that was alright. In some ways, she was grateful to be alone with her thoughts for a moment. She had so much to process. Adenike's face hovered in her mind, the expression she had when looking at the mantle. She turned and stared at it. The mantle actually had a number of interesting things on it. Some kind of glass sculpture resembling a miniature volcano that glowed orange and dimmed and then started again. Next to it was a vase of flowers with petals that looked like butterfly wings. And then there was some bizarre fish skeleton Frazyk must have preserved, maybe a souvenir or gift from Allurus.

Yes, Adenike could have been looking at any of these fascinating items, who could blame her, but somehow… Alowen looked closer at the portrait of younger Frazyk. He looked even more handsome back then, fresher faced. Was that wistfulness she had seen in Adenike's eyes, just for that moment? Did the two have some sort of…history?

Mixing work with love is not something I ever recommend.

Outside, it was raining hard. Alowen shook her head. Maybe she was overthinking. She had just met Adenike this morning, and Frazyk just two days ago. She could be making assumptions.

Well, she had better rest. She could eat lunch later and do some studying. Maybe when Frazyk came home, she could find out more about this…mystery. Alowen lay down on the plush fur while she listened to the crackling fire. Slowly, everything seemed to grow hazy around her…more and more…

There was a girl who sat in a dark room, hands on her stomach. She was carefully looking through a barely lit crack in a door, biting her lip. Alowen's heart beat.

Wait, my heart?

She looked down but there was nothing. No hands, no body. Just darkness.

I am not here!

Still, her heart was going as fast as a drum. What's going on? Then the girl shifted a little and placed a hand on her own chest. Bit by bit, the intense heartbeat slowed.

I'm feeling what she's feeling, Alowen realized.

Wherever this girl was, there were faint voices in the other room, two men talking. One of them was growing louder, repeating a certain word.

Traitor.

Alowen's eyes opened. Oh whoa, that had felt so real… She looked around and relaxed. She was back in Frazyk's cozy, classy kitchen lounge with a pink fire and rain outside. She shook her head. What in the four regions was that?!

"This day is getting stranger and stranger," Alowen murmured.

She looked at the clock, it was mid-afternoon. Frazyk wouldn't be back for at least another three hours. Her stomach rumbled. Oh goodness. She rubbed a hand over her face. If Frazyk had a couple of eggs she could fry and more coffee, she could focus on that instead of…whatever that was.

Two hours after her late lunch, Alowen looked intently over the Elemental Party guest list when the door hissed open, and Frazyk walked through the door.

"Working hard or hardly working?"

Alowen glared at him jokingly, and he laughed. "I hope you are hungry. I brought home some of those shiny fish you were so curious about."

Alowen smiled at his signature smirk and got up, stretching. The rain had long since stopped and now the sky was a dreamy, velvet purple.

"Can I help? I mean, I can gut a fish and I can certainly make a salad." She sauntered to the fridge to sort through the vegetables, grabbing an onion, an avocado, a tomato, and some lemon for the dressing. She hummed softly as she prepared a little area to work with the vegetables the way her mother would have. She felt so grown up. There had never been so much physical distance between her and her mother, yet she had never felt closer to her.

Frazyk plopped the fish down on a chopping board, rolled up his nice sleeves, and took up a knife. "I'm exhausted. The sky council can be a real pain. After dinner, I would really like to sit by the fire and tune out. Maybe watch a story on the pixilator." He pierced the fish with the knife and sawed through it. Alowen was glad he ignored her when she had offered to do the job.

"You have a pixilator?! I mean, of course you do, but I have never seen one in real life. What is it like?"

Frazyk whistled, "Never seen one? Well, words can't do it justice. You'll have to see for yourself. I think you will love it. They say someday there will be a pixilator in every home, but I rarely use mine. Being a mayor keeps one very busy, you know. Let's turn on some Wombat and let loose!"

He walked to a shelf filled with electronic contraptions, and a minute later, guitar riffs floated through the house. Chills spread first across her arms and then all the way up to the top of her head. The music was so pure and clear she felt like Wombat was in the room playing. Incredible.

Dinner was fantastic, leaving Alowen satisfied. Frazyk could grill a fine fish, she had to admit. They laughed about the council secretary reading the minutes from a meeting last year without realizing it. Frazyk explained the weird fish skeleton was actually a rare type of eel some Wolken explorers had caught swimming inside a long icicle.

But Alowen couldn't help noticing he hardly mentioned Adenike, or only glanced at her book Dexran had signed, no matter how interested his face seemed. Was this a coincidence? Later, they kicked back in front of the pixilator, and Alowen was a complete fan. Watching a story on a pixilator was like watching little colorful three-dimensional shadows, almost like little dolls acting out a story. Very unique tech.

When it was over, she peered cautiously at Frazyk. The man seemed to be lost in his own thoughts, staring quietly into the fire. She had a suspicion he had long stopped paying attention to the pixilator.

…A time when I developed a very close relationship with someone I was working on a story with. It didn't end well…

Alowen was tired but restless. She decided to go up to her room and write. Whenever she felt this way, it was hard to actually rest. Plus, there had been so little time to write her mother a letter.

"Ah, Frazyk?"

When he looked up, she told him she should probably sleep, and he nodded, giving himself a shake. "Go on, girl. You and me both. Tomorrow perhaps I could show you around Wolken a bit more."

She wished him goodnight and went upstairs. She sat, took out her favorite ink pen and some pearly sparkling stationary. But faces swirled around her. Adenike, Frazyk, Raydan, Adenike again, that girl from the strange dream, her mother, Frazyk again, Uncle Rogan, Raydan, Soren, the Water Dragon Legends book, and then Adenike once more.

And sleep took her.

The room was cool and velvet dark around Alowen as she dozed. She was only fractionally aware of the purple flames flickering across her room, keeping quiet vigil. Her mind ebbed again, and then she sunk deeper into sleep.

A girl's face appeared from the dark; the same one as before. Then the rest of her. Her knees tucked to her chest, hands on her belly, she rocked back and forth, crying softy. Her lips were mouthing, but somehow Alowen heard her voice.

Get out. Get out of here.

Deeper voices murmured behind Alowen, and she spun. But there was only light coming under some door…long shadows stretching inward, unmoving. Guards for this room? Why?

Get out of here, the girl whispered again.

Let's go together, Alowen tried to say, but she couldn't hear her own voice.

Now she couldn't see the girl fully, only her huddled silhouette. The light under the door was clear, and the shadows of the men outside. The dark seemed to thicken, pressing in closer. No. What is this? What's happening—?

And then she was back in her plush, wide bed, surrounded by walls lit with comforting purple light. Alowen felt dampness on her forehead and wiped it with the back of her hand. The only time she had felt this tired was when she had run a marathon through the trails of Blue Plum County back home. This confusing, scary dream again, twice in a row…what in Arbor was that all about? She lay there for a long time, exhausted but not enough to sleep.

***

When she woke again there was a hint of lavender dawn in the sky. At least that was calming. She lay in bed a few more moments, watching orange hues creep across the horizon. Her mom would be awake now, opening the kitchen window for a bit of fresh morning air before she started her routine sweep.

Alowen must write to her. It had been two days; she had to give her some word. Frazyk should help her get a letter home. But first, she should wash up. The wall torches silently lit before she entered the bathroom, and the air took on a minty fragrance. She splashed water on her face and looked in the mirror. The girl from the dream had looked and sounded so real. If Alowen had taken her hand, she wouldn't have been surprised to feel freezing cold skin. It was out of this world disturbing.

Perhaps she should talk to Frazyk? Her mother? Uncle Rogan? She stared into her own eyes a while longer, almost zoning out. There was just too much to think about. Then she sighed. No, if she spent another night with this dream, sure. Until then she should probably work on studying the guest list. There were, what, five days left? And no way was she going to worry her family. Her mom would instantly insist she come home, and Uncle Rogan might suggest it was nerves about the Party.

He would probably be right too. Her gaze fell on *The*

Water Dragon Legends sitting serenely on her bed. Alowen blew out a breath. She already knew the story front to back, but maybe going back to something she heard over and over during her childhood would be calming.

So, as Alowen soaked in warm bubbles and rosewater, she flipped through the pages idly. How hadn't she noticed before? Dexran never printed the Alluran prophecy following its legend. If Uncle Rogan was right, the beast would return to rid the planet of all life once again on another new moon, and the only hope of stopping it was finding its master, who alone could coax the beast back into the ocean. Apparently, a new era would follow, one where the four elements would gradually merge into one different race.

Huh. Weird how Allurus would only allow the legend to be printed, not the prophecy. Maybe they didn't like the idea of merging with the other races. She wondered what Dexran did to get printing rights at all. Oh well. At least the distraction helped her frazzled mind.

As she got up, her body felt sore but that was probably all the excitement. She sighed and breathed in mint air. It was a new day in Wolken.

She was brushing her teeth when her eyes fell on the bottle of eagle talon essence from yesterday. Alowen frowned as she picked it up. It didn't actually look all that old, probably a year at most. She hadn't seen Frazyk with a girlfriend or anything. His house was empty—she was sure now after living with him two days. Surely he couldn't be so busy he wouldn't have someone. It was probably not her business, but still…Frazyk didn't seem like the lonesome bachelor type.

She walked back into the bedroom. It was now light blue outside, and the first eagles of the day sailed across the air amongst a couple of electric orbs. Frazyk mentioned taking her around Wolken, so maybe today they'd get to ride one.

She tingled with anticipation as she headed downstairs. Sure, she did say she would work hard, but yesterday was spent indoors, and she still hadn't seen that much of the city.

"There she is." Frazyk greeted when she entered the kitchen. "Well rested, ready for the day!"

His pensiveness from last evening was gone. He had another guest today, a woman younger than him and Adenike, but older than Alowen. She was dressed very differently too, in a black jacket lined with sharp, silver stripes over a shirt bearing the image of a gazelle's head. A black cap was perched smartly at an angle on her reddish-brown hair.

Frazyk clapped the woman on the shoulder. "Alowen, say 'hi' to your personal shopper, Leena!"

Leena smiled and put her hand out to shake. She was short for a Wolkenian, just five-eight, but her grip was firm and confident.

"Good to meet you, Alowen! I brought breakfast, too."

A basket of pears and grapes sat on the table, along with bread and a disc of white cheese. Frazyk was going eagerly at the grapes, making his way through them with quick bites.

"Have one. Frazyk is making short work of them." Leena held out a grape of such a deep purple it almost looked black. When Alowen bit into it, sweet juice flooded her mouth. Frazyk chuckled at the way her eyes widened.

"They grow these just a few miles inland from Allurus water. Apparently, the white cliffs on the coastline cushion their grapevines from the sea wind nicely." He wiped his fingers on a towel, and then clapped his hands. "Leena has been away shopping for other Party guests, but today she's back to figure out your outfit. I just need to be at my office this morning, and then we are going on a small tour of Wolken later."

"Oh!" Alowen blurted, then covered her mouth. "I'm sorry, didn't mean to interrupt." Frazyk waved it off amusedly, and she cleared her throat. "I just wanted to know if I can get a letter home to my mom."

Frazyk nodded. "We can take it to the post office anytime, don't worry. Today if you like. Amidst all this excitement"—he wagged his finger at her mock sternly—"I want you to study hard this evening, yes? The Party is only five days away now."

Alowen giggled, half grateful, half nervous.

"Don't mind him, Alowen. He tries to be chipper, but deep down he's a worrier," Leena said, generously spreading cheese on bread.

She nudged Alowen and laughed aloud at Frazyk's snort. Alowen wanted to laugh, too. It wasn't every day someone teased Frazyk. But he shook his head good-naturedly. "Hmph. Don't you corrupt her! One of you is bad enough. I'll be back by lunch, Alowen."

When he left, Alowen took Leena's hand. "I forgot to thank you for the beautiful dress two days ago. It really made me look good. I can't be grateful enough."

"Don't mention it." Leena opened a notebook, revealing pages on pages of neat colorful sketches. "When Frazyk and your uncle showed me your picture and measurements, I knew it would be just right on you. But with the Party, we can't buy any old thing out there. We have to design it. Thankfully, I have a tailor friend who can make the most brilliant things under pressure." She flipped to a certain page and slid the book to Alowen. "What do you think?"

"Oh, wow!" It was such an accurate drawing of her in a gown as green as a dragonfly with tiny gold daffodils on the sleeves and around the collar. Leena had even added an orange gem pendant, labeled "amber."

"I really like the gold and amber against the green."

Leena made a face. "It does match your eyes, but it's missing something. Here, have some breakfast while I fine-tune another sketch."

The bread was still delightfully warm, toasted with sun-flower seeds, and the cheese was supple, almost creamy. Alowen could eat it the whole day.

Finally, Leena tapped on a new drawing.

"White blouse and green skirt, with a brooch of a red vase on the breast. People will know you to be from the Arbor, much more friendly and approachable."

Each region had a distinctive icon. The Arbor with its vase symbolizing the humble, grounded clay that made a lot of things. Wolken with its saddle, always traveling. Bachha with its conch shell. Allurus with its bright, coral starfish, something they kept bringing up from the seabed for some light trade. Alowen thought for a bit. The Arbor icon would align with her approach of being friendly and receptive to people, and she never would have thought a clay vase of all things would make her so nostalgic, but she had to think clearly...

"What if there were other Arbor guests there? Will I stand out?"

Leena nodded. "You are right. It's a minimalistic look... but yes, we don't want you blending in too much. Alright, try this one. This was done just yesterday." This third one was a satin, purple dress with ruffs of small white feathers and a pearl brooch of a quill. "For our Party scribe, eh?"

Alowen blinked, barely hearing her. Leena had drawn excellently for all three, but this... Not too heavy on the feathers, but nothing plain either. "I want it."

Leena paused. "You do...?"

"It is me. I am a writer and that's what I'm bringing to this party. I want people to know I am from the Arbor from the way I talk and how much I care, not just from a brooch." As she said the words, she knew it was the right pick.

Leena clapped quietly. "Well said, scribe. Well said. You

sound more mature than your age." She ticked the page and stood. "I'll get this to my tailor friend now, but I'll be back a day before the Party." She smirked. "If you weren't so young, I'm sure we could deck you out in something more freeing. Let the snobs stare."

Alowen smiled. Leena didn't seem like any other Wolkenian, even Frazyk. Where he teased around topics with hints and subtlety, she seemed to bluntly mock-insult and challenge, yet more charming than rude.

"Frazyk said not to corrupt me, remember?"

"Oh, him!" Leena tilted her cap this way and that. "Get some booze in that one, and he'll be looser than me. Oh hey"—she turned—"Speaking of being loose, keep an eye out for Sal and his entourage, yeah?"

Alowen turned pink. "I haven't read my guest list yet. Who are they?"

"Oh, I hear Sal got himself added last minute so maybe he won't be on your list. He's one of the most handsome ambassadors from Allurus who convinced his superiors to try something new this year." Leena shrugged. "I hear he's representing a more…progressive community to show the world Allurus in a different light, so he'll have a number of young Alluran folks around him at the Party. Some talents, some with interesting ideas." She waggled her fingers. "How exciting, eh? Bye!"

Alowen laughed, waving. She felt lighter, more relaxed. The room felt emptier and duller without Leena. Her mom would be shocked to meet this woman. Oh, her mom! She should write that letter now before Frazyk came back. She found some pen and paper, and for the next hour, she wrote.

Mom,

How are you? I miss you so much! I'm sorry it has taken me so long to write. How is everything? How is Uncle Rogan? How are the animals? Frazyk's house is lovely! I have met some interesting people (some dull people as well). It is so different here. Most people are so tall, and almost everything is so fancy. Thankfully, I have made some friends who've been getting me ready for the Party. I miss the Arbor, but I know I made the right decision coming here. I don't know if I will ever be truly prepared for the Element Party, but I have to try to follow my heart and be myself. I can leave the Arbor, but the Arbor won't leave me. Maybe if I try being out in "the world" first and it doesn't work out, I can at least appreciate being home. I hope you know how much I love you and how much I appreciate having you as a mother.

This whole business of being an adult is tougher than I thought! Anyways, expect to get some souvenirs when I get to Bachha. Give Uncle Rogan a hug for me. Stay warm, I know it's getting cold there.

Xoxo,

Alowen

Alowen sat back and shook her hand, sore from gripping the pen. After so many rewrites, she was finally satisfied. And not a moment too soon. There was the beat of wings outside, and Frazyk came in a minute later, humming.

"Well, my clerk is handling the rest of the work this afternoon. Filing papers, sorting folders," he exaggerated a yawn. "Hungry? Let's have lunch outside, and then we'll mail your letter. Come, there are some gorgeous places to see!"

"Can't wait."

Alowen tingled excitedly as she pocketed the letter. When they mounted Tyrq and took off, the sun warmed her back, but the wind cooled her brow. She didn't realize how much a day indoors would make her miss flying. Each time she felt a bit less nervous, able to take in more of the city. It spread out below her, a bed of silver spires, marble sculptures, and glass towers. It was like looking at a board game. But then Tyrq flew lower, and she could take in Wolken up close. She hadn't seen the beautiful streams cascading all through the city before but decided they must be man-made. They were so perfectly placed. Some flowed rapidly, others slower. One or two were green, like gems, but many twinkled in the sun. Anywhere they intersected with pedestrians, she saw bridges and parks with opalescent benches nearby. Many people ate lunch near the water. Some even had blankets spread out for a picnic. Another pang of homesickness welled inside as she remembered picnics back in the Arbor with friends and family.

It was a very popular pastime there. Most social activities there took place outside. Even in the winter they built snow forts and had snowball fights or invented games like ice skate tag (she had accumulated quite a few bruises with that one). Alowen suddenly realized she hadn't noticed any children roaming the streets. Then she remembered Wolken had very strict schools. Most children went to school for almost twelve hours a day and had to participate in a minimum of two sports and two fine arts. She couldn't imagine what that would have been like. In the Arbor, they were free to choose whether they wanted any extracurriculars. They only had class for seven hours a day. Whenever the weather permitted, teachers would hold classes outside.

It was an effort not to cry, but the wind dried her eyes anyway. They flew over cafes, gardens, some kind of grooming salon for eagles, even a giant stone seahorse who spouted water into a fountain, but Tyrq seemed to be heading toward the edge of the city. Finally, they alighted on a massive, round platform protruding from the side of the wall with a meadow, of all things. Broad umbrella trees lined the sides, casting shade over most of the place. On one end of the platform stood a ranch house that appeared to be smooth stone. It was a blue-gray that reminded her of the sky after a storm and the windows were perfectly round. It was so different from the humble wood homes in the Arbor. There were even a couple of cattle pens. No wonder this place was on the edge of Wolken! It would have looked so out of place much more inward.

As Tyrq swooped lower, she saw tiny brown flashes dart across the grass. Most vanished, but one was too slow. Tyrq dove like lightning, pinning it.

"A rabbit!" Alowen cried.

She had never seen an eagle catch anything before.

"It's alright," Frazyk said. "The rabbits here are meant for our eagles to catch and kill, to give them a chance to be the predators they are. The people who built the ranch were from the Arbor, actually. They wanted things natural which is why they chose stone instead of cloud crystal." He patted Tyrq on the head. "You know the rules, my friend. Wait until we are gone." Sure enough, the eagle waited for them to dismount and walk up to the ranch before Alowen saw him bend down. "Mr. Loggerman has lived in Wolken most of his life," Frazyk commented. "But like his dad, grills things up Arbor style." Rabbits in their path scattered. Somewhere ahead, a cow bellowed. "He only butchers his cows twice a year though, so it's rare. Most of the time he uses Wolken goats on the side of the mountains. Much more plentiful. Not as authentic as your mother's food, but for us Wolkenians, close enough."

Alowen's stomach grumbled. "I'll be the true judge of Mr. Loggerman's cooking today."

Frazyk gasped dramatically. "Oh my, watch out! She's on the warpath today."

Alowen huffed. "What can I say? Arbor people get grouchy being two days from home."

It turned out Mr. Loggerman was surprisingly up to the challenge of frying up a mean burger with greasy onions and crunchy lettuce. He would have served them goat, but upon hearing Alowen was from the Arbor, he brought out his best beef.

"It's hard to keep them fed Arbor style," he admitted. "Most of the year I have to keep them fed on grain while I try growing proper grass with seeds from the Arbor. My old man wanted it that way."

On the inside, his ranch looked just the way an Arbor one would have with timber log walls, long dark wood tables, and even an old-fashioned hearth. Alowen's heart and stomach were full as she looked around the home away from home. She decided to come back and ask if he would like to join her when she left for home.

Frazyk paid for the meal, and Tyrq's rabbit, before they strolled back across the meadow. He was humming merrily, hands in his pockets, happy to watch Alowen connect with her roots. But what about his own?

"Frazyk, can I ask you a question? It's sort of personal." He looked at her, eyebrows raised.

"Ask away. You are here to learn how to do that, no?" One of his eyes looked sparkly yellow in the sun.

"Very funny," she muttered, but the joke softened her nerves. She really didn't want to upset him. Alright, here it went. "Frazyk, you live by yourself, but have you always? Where is your family?"

"Mm…," he mused as if choosing his words. "My parents passed on long ago, and I was an only child. When I was younger, I had roommates and friends. We had good times, trust me." He grinned. "But ah"—he stepped over a rabbit that froze to watch his long legs—"turns out the Mayor of

Wolken gets a place all to himself."

"Have you ever wanted to change that, to have a family? Have you ever been in love?" This time Frazyk took longer to speak. Alowen held her breath.

"Yes, I was in love once. Once." They walked a bit further before he shrugged and smiled at her. "It was a good adventure while it lasted."

Maybe it was from the past few days of living with him, but this smile looked a bit more forced.

"What happened? Why didn't you marry her?"

"Life had other plans," Frazyk said simply. "But there's more to life than romance and family. You are still young; you'll learn this very soon. Put down roots and a lot of things get harder. Travel, adventures"—he winked—"seeing the world?"

"I don't know…" She could only think of her parents. It seemed like love was hard enough to come by without letting the world rip it away from you. Alowen's mother was happy enough, but she never looked at another man after Alowen's father died. She had Uncle Rogan, but Alowen wondered if it was lonely for her. "Don't you want to have someone to look forward to when you come home?"

"Oh…once upon a time." Tyrq was in view now, looking right at them over the grass. "But when you are both up and rising, you figure out quickly that love doesn't mix well with that. Wolken culture, I'm afraid." Before she could respond, Frazyk looked up to the sky, shading his eyes. "Come, we'll mail your letter, and there's a pretty garden with a lake I want to show you. A lot of artists visit there. And then we have a brilliant library you'll just want to stay at forever. Come, come!"

Gregon Barlow…Celia Hare…Droven Ewing…

Alowen stretched, opening her eyes slowly to golden light dancing off the walls of her bedroom. Only four more days until the Element Party. She felt a knot in her stomach, but another thought had her sitting up straight. No dream and no girl last night. What did it mean? Alowen rubbed one eye drowsily. Maybe she was too tired from studying all evening.

She chuckled but only half-heartedly. That guest list was no game. Every attendant had such long, elaborate careers and at least four fascinating anecdotes. She had stayed up with strong coffee reading so much her head still swam with names. A part of her related to the feeling of being trapped. Maybe the dream was just her worries and stress manifesting? Even with her lifelong wishes coming true, even with the wonder of touring Wolken yesterday, she had to admit sometimes she felt like a prisoner.

Life held so many expectations, what if she couldn't follow through? All those names to remember, all those questions to plan and practice. At least she had some sort of plan: get through half the list by today, then the rest tomorrow. Adenike would be pleased, hopefully. But what if she failed? It seemed like there was more freedom without expectations. Apparently, there was a man in the Arbor who lived alone on the edge of the woods. It didn't make sense if the rumors were right about him being part water and part fire because the forest had neither element. Alowen was never sure she really believed the tales, which claimed he didn't really have any friends, just a pet raven who kept guard outside his house. Or claimed that he was exiled for murder. Either way, if he was even real, he was away from responsibilities.

No sense lamenting her mini-existential crisis in bed. The dreams had stopped; there's no need to tell anyone. She had work to do. She slipped out of bed and got dressed. Peach cardigan, white pants, a simple pretty look. The colors reminded her of the Gallery of Wolken West where Frazyk had taken her yesterday. One display boasted a garish sandcastle of pink cloud crystals mixed with special violet sand grains, and another showed off a master tailor's snowy bridal gown with silver sequins glittering against alpaca wool.

Alowen raised her eyebrows at the mirror. The intense studying had driven away their conversation, but somehow she couldn't forget it. Much as she admired Frazyk, and as happy as he seemed now, he just seemed to be missing something.

She gathered her notes and stepped into the hallway. It was also possible he had other women in his past, but he did talk about Adenike with that certain look in his eye…

Oh well. She'd have to think about it later.

You are still young; you'll learn this very soon. Put down roots and a lot of things get harder. Travel, adventures, seeing the world?

Maybe Frazyk had the right idea. Maybe life was just freer not being in a committed relationship. Maybe.

Frazyk had left two cloud berry scones, a note, and a recipe book on the kitchen counter:

At work. Meet Adenike at Star Café at 1 pm. I stuck a map and the house key in this book. Get to know the city better!

She cracked a smile. Maybe later if she had the time. Adenike would want to go over some of her questions and maybe her delivery. She swallowed and shuffled through her notes.

Daray Brascott…Tranton Volk…Lila Shale…

Perhaps she ought to get familiar with the directions first. Who knew how these Wolken streets were? She slid the recipe book toward her. Sure enough, the slim, dark, brass key was right beneath the cover. Frazyk must have been in a rush this morning judging by the wad of papers there with it. Alowen sighed, shuffling through them like a deck of cards. Receipts, memos, old council minutes, but no map…

Finally, she saw the corner of a map and pulled it out, relieved. Several other things slid out with it. More receipts and even news clippings. Alowen couldn't help but catch some of their titles. An eagle race around the peaks of Wolken Hills. The opening of a new goat's cheese restaurant outside the city. And then under all that, there was one dated fifteen years back, headlined with big, bold fonts:

SCANDAL - MAYOR DROW HUMILIATED; DAUGHTER FOUND ROMANTICALLY ENTANGLED WITH MIXED-ELEMENT PAINTER, TENNO MORICE

Alowen scowled. Under this last news clipping was a simple note. It looked like Adenike's handwriting.

Frazyk, look at this. It's getting serious. Tenno told me he's been getting hate mail everywhere. He's leaving the city today, and I hear the mayor has sent his daughter to boarding school somewhere outside Allurus. I am scared, Frazyk.

Alowen sat for a long time and stared at the two items. Was Adenike in a relationship with someone back then?

What position was Frazyk in then? Or maybe…Could it be? She frowned at the note again. It's possible…

The kitchen clock chimed, and she jumped. Oh, she was still an hour early, but that was okay. Walking the streets to Star Café would give her time to process and prepare for today's lesson. Something made her slip the news clipping and the note into her bag with just a bit of guilt. Frazyk had long forgotten about this, she told herself. Right…?

The sunlight and outside views were a welcome distraction. The clothes people wore here were breathtaking on the Wolkenian tall frames, cascading down along the shimmering sidewalks. One woman wore a floor-length dress that reminded her of the shimmering scales of a fish. Whenever it caught the light, the color shifted like the rainbow prisms of a crystal whenever sunlight shone through it.

A few streets and blocks later, she stepped inside the café. There was a giant fireplace casting a warm peach light along the wall on the right filled with books. Above it a sign read, "Please feel free to take a book with you. We accept donated books as well." What a great idea. Plush chairs in dark-hued fabrics filled the room.

It was mostly empty, other than a slightly plump woman wearing a very startling orange hat behind the counter. She looked more like someone from the Arbor. Alowen ordered a sage tea and took a seat in the back where she could still see the door. Soft violin with a trace of oboe wafted through the store. The windows had thick, slate metal frames that reminded her of the restaurants back in the Arbor. The more she looked around, the more she thought it likely the woman was from the Arbor. Her café had such heavy nature themes. The furniture was all made of thick wood. Sculptures of bright red mushrooms with white polka dots hung on the walls. A forest mural spanned the entire left side of the café. A deer stood in the center drinking from a creek, shaded by oaks and pines.

Then her eyes closed.

When they opened again the girl was right next to her. They stood at another window, small and round. Alowen glanced out into a haze of water and saw a sprawling, sandy landscape. There were giant coral structures and schools of fish swimming by. The girl's arms were a pale green, the skin of the Water People. This was Allurus.

Someone knocked on the door behind her and a short woman walked in carrying a plate of fish. The girl jumped as she knelt in front of her.

"Princess Ilya? It's me. Are you well?"

"Jez?" The girl's voice came out weakly. "Where's— where's Lei?"

"Shh…shh…" The woman's voice dropped though somehow Alowen could still hear her. "He's out in Bachha now, Princess. He's finishing his plans. When the time comes for the Party presentation, I'll come with more details. But please, hush now. I can't tell you anymore. You must eat this, or you'll get sick."

The woman, Jez, placed the plate on the floor. Ilya's hands shook as she tore off tiny pieces of fish and brought them to her mouth. Her face was pained as she swallowed.

Jez got up. "I am very sorry, Princess."

She left, and a guard slammed the door behind her. The princess tried again to eat. She had to be starving, but she was clearly in a great despair. She fell to her knees crying.

The long, low sound of oboe broke through from the background. Alowen refocused on the forest mural, trying to imagine herself amongst the comforting dark pines. She thought of all the times she had heard a creek flowing, how relaxing the sound was. She noticed a group of brightly colored mushrooms off to the side and began counting the bright white polka dots on the red caps. She had learned from her school counselor back in the Arbor that counting objects could sometimes calm anxiety. Still, her stomach was turning a bit, and she grabbed the heavy, wooden table to steady herself. Just when she thought she was done with those visions…

Questions swirled in her head. Who was this girl? Who's Lei and what plan was this? What did they have to do with the Party? Why couldn't she eat the fish? From what Uncle Rogan told her, the people of Allurus mostly ate a diet of raw fish with just a bit of seaweed. This time she wasn't even asleep. There really had to be something to these visions.

She took a sip of her steaming sage tea, an Arbor staple. The earthy aroma immediately carried her back to her mother's kitchen. She could see the bright copper teapot on the familiar stove, steam pouring from the spout.

"Alowen! Hello, young miss!" She jumped as she looked back at the door. Adenike was there, grinning from ear to ear. Her teeth were so white they almost had their own light. "Frazyk asked me to pick these up for you to take to the party. It's only a few days away! Are you excited?" She set the packages down—a sleek leather-bound journal and a small black satchel with straps and put up a hand to order some tea of her own.

Alowen blushed, pushing the visions as far back in her mind as possible. Better for Adenike not to glimpse what's going on in her head. Unfortunately, that made her focus on the items in front of her. She had a hard time accepting gifts from people.

"You guys have done so much for me. I don't know if I could have been prepared without you. Thank you. To answer your question, yes, I am excited. Right now, I am still more nervous than excited, but I guess the only way to learn to swim is to jump in the water, right? Well, anyways, that's what my uncle always says."

"Dear Alowen, I am more than happy to offer you any help I can. Come, Frazyk told me how much you had been studying and I'm so proud! Let's look at your questions. Let's start here with Gregon Barlow at the top of your list."

Alowen pulled out her notes.

"Well, Gregon's father owned a horse stable in the Arbor where he spent most of his time as a child. He's very busy with his speaking—author engagements in Wolken—but I can ask him about his family stables. If he still rides horses and which was his favorite? Maybe talking about what helps him relax may get him to open up a bit."

"That's a good start, Alowen! It looks like you have some follow-ups that let you ease into his upcoming speaking arrangements and his next book." Adenike stirred honey into her tea and took a sip. "Okay, what do you have here for Celia Hare? As you've read, this one was a bit more difficult. She's managed to keep the media out of her personal life."

Alowen sat up straight. "Would it be too direct to ask her how she manages to keep her life such a mystery when she performs in Bachha every weekend?" She frowned. Had she botched this question?

"Oh, I've heard ruder questions, but you can word it gently and throw in a compliment, so she receives it well. Something along the lines of 'with thousands attending your shows each weekend, you've still managed to keep your privacy. That takes skill, especially for a performing actress of fifteen years. How do you manage to keep your private life away from public eye?'" She waved toward Alowen. "Give it a try."

Alowen cleared her throat. "With thousands of…"

The next hour flew by. Adenike had Alowen practice her smile, her eye contact, even how to sit without tensing. They went over her questions again, then body language. They ordered more tea and then back to questions.

Finally, Alowen sat back, letting out a breath.

"Wow. Am I glad you came by to help me practice. Delivering these questions confidently is harder than I thought!"

Adenike laughed. "You remind me of myself when I was first chosen. Before you go into that elaborate banquet hall, just remember to take three deep breaths. Make sure your stomach is fully extended, then breathe out as slow as you can. Pull your shoulders down away from your ears. These are just people, important people yes, but just people. They all get nervous. They've had hard days and good days, just like you."

Alowen took a deep breath and sat up straight with her shoulders back. Adenike clapped. "Yes! Just like that. You'll find yourself much more natural than you think, I promise."

Alowen sipped her tea. Oops, cold. "And if I can't stay calm, you'll be there, right?"

Silence. Adenike coughed into her fist. "Well, I won't see you again before you leave. I am actually going out of town on business."

"Oh no!" Alowen felt her heart sink. "What am I going to do without you?"

Her throat tightened, her head felt lighter, and the room spun a bit. "Look at how much practice I needed. What if I genuinely can't do this, Adenike? What if I try to ask someone at the party a question and only say nonsense? Or worse, what if I accidentally insult someone? Maybe I've overestimated myself—"

"Hey, hey." Adenike reached across the table and took her hand. The warmth brought Alowen some relief. "This is a lot. Anyone in your situation would feel afraid. When I was preparing to be a scribe, I was so nervous I lost three pounds in a week and a half. I remember waking up the middle of every night covered in sweat. The truth is everyone understands scribes are brand new to all of this. That's the charm of having scribes come to Bachha straight from school, it's disarming. No one expects you to be an expert and it's okay if you make mistakes. I wish I could go back and tell myself to relax and be myself. You were chosen because you are a great writer, and you are warm, and lovely to talk to." She squeezed Alowen's hand. "Believe in yourself, please, because I do. Ten years from now when you are successful in whatever path you choose, I hope you look back at this moment with pride. You are doing so well."

"I—I don't know what to say. Thank you." Tears welled up. "I don't think I realized how much pressure I was putting on myself."

Adenike leaned forward and looked Alowen in the eye. "Your dedication is beautiful, and makes you, you. But just like I did, you'll learn to balance that pressure with patience and compassion. This world is brand new for you. In time, it'll feel like an old glove, and you'll walk into any room confidently. But for now, it's okay to acknowledge this is scary! Please promise me you will get in touch with me, and let's have tea after the Element Party. I can't wait to hear how well it went." A reassuring smile spread across her face.

"Okay." Alowen shook her head. She took a deep breath and blew up toward her eyes to dry her tears. "You are right, you're right. I've worked hard for this. And tea after the Element Party would be amazing. I'm sure to have some wild stories for you."

"Here, let's take a break," Adenike pushed their notes aside. "I brought good news. How would you like to know where you are staying?"

"Would I?" It felt good to chuckle again. "I almost forgot. It better be something fancy!" she joked.

Every year, the Party organizers tried rotating between locales for the Party guests. It's a wonder they hadn't run out of places yet, but Bachha was that huge.

"That's right, girl, wish it into being! This past year, Bachha has been upgrading its nicest hotel, the Conche, so everyone's going back in there." Adenike laughed at her stunned face. "The stay of a lifetime!"

"The Conche??" Alowen gasped.

The Party was extravagant, yes, but it looked like the organizers' limits were high above hers. Even B-list celebrities struggled to get a spot there, that was how lavish exclusive the Conche was. "They are really pulling out all the stops, aren't they?"

"Girl, you have no idea." Adenike winked. "I only wish I could watch your face when you see it. But I tried to snoop for you yesterday, and you're on the sixth floor with purple lighting. The valet at the entrance won't give me any more details though, I'm sorry."

"Well, purple is actually one of my favorite colors so that's good enough for me." Alowen ran her hand through her hair. "I know my mind is probably going to melt when I take it all in."

"Hey, remember." Adenike demonstrated by taking an exaggerated deep breath and pulling her shoulders down.

Alowen pulled her shoulders down and away too. *It's just people.*

"You're going to be just fine, Alowen." Adenike's eyes sparkled. She seemed to be enjoying Alowen facing her upcoming experiences. Adenike would be a fantastic mother, Alowen realized. Calming, worldly. She could show her children how to tap into the world.

"Now, one last thing." Adenike pulled a tape recorder from her bag. "Have you used one of these before?"

Mr. Blaught always had her class practice interviewing each other with tape recorders. "I have used one for school projects."

"This will save your life when you are interviewing." She

briefly tapped the record button and then played back her own voice. Then she rewound to erase. "Make sure it's on, even when you are writing down the details. You will be surprised what you miss, not to mention how many fantastic pieces have been ruined by a spilled cup of coffee. It helps to have backup."

"Good idea, I will probably get too excited and forget to write something down anyways. I will feel more comfortable listening to it again later in my room." She picked it up and slid it into her satchel. "This one's heavier than what school used!"

"It's a news station standard-grade model. You'll get used to the weight." Adenike winked again. Wait—how had she missed it before? Frazyk tilted his head the same way. No, she had to be overthinking. Her emotions were all over the place today. But before she could process it, Adenike stood.

"Well, I need to run and pack for my trip, and I see our local fog coming in from the city borders, so come, let's clear up quick."

Alowen rose and after gathering their things, walked out, and hugged at the door. Adenike was right, a pure white fog had slowly inched up the street. They had better be fast if they didn't want to get swallowed. Adenike's grip was stronger than Alowen expected, as though she really didn't want to let go. Her eyes teared up a second time, but she didn't want Adenike to see, so she blew her breath at her eyes again and tilted her head back to wipe her eyes while she pretended to sneeze.

"Thank you so much."

Adenike looked her square in the face, her smile gentle and proud. "I have all the faith in the world you will do a fantastic job this weekend. Remember to relax, breathe, and be yourself."

With a wave, Adenike turned and walked into the fog. Clutching her satchel, Alowen trudged back to Frazyk's house, determined to take a nap. All of these emotions had worn her out.

"So, what do you think?" came Leena's voice from behind as Alowen turned this way and that before the mirror.

Leena's sketch had come to life. The white feathers shimmered like snow in the light, creating a cascading effect over the shoulders, neck, and waist of the plum-hued satin emphasizing her curves. The satin fabric shone like water at night. Alowen pinned the pearl quill to her breast, and it winked. She had even inserted her mom's pearl stud earrings.

"I really love this dress. Leena, you are so talented." She had made sure to deal with her hair earlier. "Everything just looks so sleek together!"

"Glad you think so." Leena walked up with a satisfied smirk from the wall she was leaning against. "My friend and I worked our butts off these past couple days, but this makes it all worth it."

"Wow, Leena! You have really outdone yourself this time!" Frazyk let out a low whistle. Alowen felt herself blush. "That purple really suites you, Alowen."

"I live to serve, Mayor." Alowen had never seen anyone do a curtsy in wide-legged pants before, but Leena pulled it off gracefully.

"I shall see you both at the Party. So much of my handiwork in one place, all those celebrities wearing my suggestions. Alowen, you know how to stash that dress, remember how I showed you. Steam it thoroughly when you hang it up in your room. Later!" She sauntered out.

Frazyk joined Alowen at the mirror as she waved. "You will draw every eye at the Party, trust me." He wiped an imaginary tear from his eye. "They grow up so fast."

Alowen rolled her eyes jokingly, but she had to admit Frazyk's relaxedness helped. The next two days flew by almost too quickly. She had gone over all the names, memorized key parts of every anecdote, even watched some pixilator documentaries of some of their lives. She had gone over the Party program at least three times a day. She had practiced talking in the mirror and with Frazyk until she could speak without stammering. But today was where it counted. Today she would leave for Bachha.

"I know it will be fine, but I'm just so afraid I will embarrass myself." She fiddled nervously with one of her earrings and looked to Frazyk. His knowing smile didn't flinch.

"Nerves are normal, Alowen. You've done all the necessary preparation. As for the average person, there will be far too much commotion for people to notice any social faux pas on your part. Most of the time people are so concerned with their own worries they hardly notice the world around them. The sooner you realize this the more you will relax. Here, take this lemon lip gloss." He handed her the tube. "Now change out of your dress and we'll have breakfast." He turned to the kitchen. "Food makes one feel grounded. I'll make toast in just a second."

Alowen's hands shook as she hurried upstairs. She had left a simple shirt, pants, and a tan sweater her mother knitted out on the bed along with her suitcase and some rose water. Carefully, she slipped out of the beautiful dress and started to fold it into a small space at the top of her suitcase, just the way Leena had shown her. This time she tried not to look in the mirror as she put on the other clothes. For every big event, she always got so nervous she never felt satisfied with her appearance. Instead, she closed the rose water spray and slid it into her new black bag. That way if her sweating got out of hand, she had a quick solution. She checked the bag again and made sure her pencils, journal, and tape recorder were in place. Finally, she slipped Frazyk's lip gloss into her pocket.

She took one more look around the purple-lit room, her throat tightening. She'd carefully stacked the bed high with fluffy white pillows and had to fight the urge to crawl back in. She took one last glance in the bathroom, breathing in its fragrant mist—honeysuckle today. She was going to miss her morning and evening soaks in this large crystal bathtub where she could just let go of her worries. One day she would get a bathtub like it. She closed her eyes tightly to memorize every detail and then turned.

After she hauled her things downstairs, she felt better over a plate of eggs, cheese, and peppers. Frazyk was right, food really did have that grounding effect. Sometimes she forgot to eat under stress, a habit she really must break.

"So, how are we getting to Allurus? Are we leaving soon?"

"Ooh my." Frazyk waved a piece of toast at her with a wink. "Today's your lucky day because we are finally taking an electric orb. Let's finish up, it's almost time to go."

An electric orb? Alowen felt a fizzle of excitement. One more thing she could check off her list of Wolken experiences. When they had put away everything, she slipped on her satchel and shifted her luggage to the door. Frazyk already waited outside gently tapping his foot beside Tyrq. It struck her as odd before she remembered how Adenike had empathized with her. Maybe Frazyk was also nervous and reliving pieces of his youth. He smiled, huge and genuine. There was something in his eyes she hadn't seen before, almost like pride.

"Alowen, I know it's only been a few days, and I don't want to get all sappy on you, but I want you to know you are almost like a daughter to me. If you don't make sure to write every once in a while, after the Party, I will most likely cry myself to sleep and eat large pints of cloud berry ice cream."

There was the wink, one last time for good measure. She giggled as she hugged him. Of course, she would keep in touch. Together, they hoisted their bags onto Tyrq.

Alowen had a thought as Frazyk picked up Tyrq's harness. "Wait, let me saddle him." Frazyk looked amused. "Well, well. Looks like you're as comfortable with him now as I am. You've come a long way, hasn't she, Tyrq?"

The eagle's only response was to pin an unblinking yellow gaze on her. This time she bravely held his gaze, willing herself to stay calm. Several long moments passed, but eventually, the eagle blinked and looked away, seeming bored. Oh well, at least she dared to try this time. Maybe she'd never get it.

She ground her teeth and kept working on her buckles. Finally, she stepped back to admire her work, dusting her hands.

"How's that?"

Frazyk gave her a smile. "Couldn't have done better myself."

Alowen let him lift her up into the front saddle. A week ago, she wouldn't have believed she could saddle, let alone ride a giant eagle. "Up, up and away!"

Frazyk made a grand arm gesture, probably more his silliness than any proper direction for Tyrq. The eagle always seemed to know what to do. Even as the wind picked up around them, Tyrq launched and swept forward calmly.

Alowen herself felt a stillness inside. It was finally game time. Everything felt surreal, almost like the world was in slow motion. Below her, the spires of the cloud buildings lit up like jewels in the sunlight. The parks throughout the city were already busy as brightly colored capes and hats walked along the pathways and sat at the tiny tables for breakfast. She thought she caught a glimpse of Sielo, but the sign was so tiny from this distance she couldn't be sure. A tear ran down her cheek as Frazyk's tower dwindled behind them. She hadn't realized it, but over the days it had begun to feel like a home away from home.

As if the world was easing along her farewell, a thick front of fog moved in over streets and parks and blocks. Finally, surrounded by white, she closed her eyes for a moment and felt the cold air rush past her.

As they flew, Alowen thought about the first time she was on Tyrq's back. She wouldn't see Tyrq again until after the week's festivities and she was on her way back to the Arbor. For the first time, she wondered what lay ahead after the Element Party. Many people began illustrious careers once their scribe duties were over. Who knows who she would meet and what would happen?

Ten years from now when you are successful in whatever path you choose, I hope you look back at this moment with pride.

Another time, she thought.

The girl's face crept back in small flashes, but they were fainter this time. Either she hadn't had any more visions, or maybe she just couldn't remember her dreams. She lay her head on the soft leather bag in front of her and closed her eyes. The wind felt so soothing on her face and for a moment she was at peace. No visions, no questions. They were a product of her stress, nothing more.

"Please land on spot seventeen!"

The next thing she felt was a bump beneath her. She opened her eyes and they had landed on a steel deck with neat, numbered rectangles. Many of these were occupied with people dismounting from eagles or unsaddling them. Some people in beige uniforms unloaded baggage from the backs of several eagles. One step below was a broader deck packed with dense crowds. At the far end, pink and orange flashes caught her eye as electric orbs floated in and took off. It struck her how truly beautiful they were, even against the cloudy sky. People were shuffling into lines in front of each one.

"Mayor Frazyk!" She looked around as an attendant wheeled a set of portable steps towards them. "So pleased to see you today. May I take your saddle and harness?"

"Be my guest, young man."

Frazyk was already on the deck, unbuckling her bags. Almost in a daze, Alowen swung a leg over Tyrq's back and went down the steps placed below. As soon as her feet touched the deck, the attendant unstrapped the harness in smooth, fast motions and took it away with the steps. Alowen stared.

"Oh, he'll deliver it to my house. My address is already in their system," Frazyk said casually. He gave Tyrq's chest a fond pat. "Take care, dear friend." The eagle seemed to glance ever so slightly at Alowen before he lifted off with a ruffle of feathers. "Tyrq is going to miss you, Alowen. I can see it in his eyes." Frazyk let out a chuckle, "Alright, this way."

With one last look at Tyrq's vanishing form, Alowen turned and followed Frazyk into the crowd. The throng was packed densely around her. The shortest of them were almost a full foot taller than her but everyone looked so polite; they didn't look intimidating. People were staring at

Frazyk, some smiled and waved, others whispered, looking star-struck.

"There used to be a mayoral orb," Frazyk whispered as they smiled and nudged through the throng. "But I felt uncomfortable having my personal orb and loading station, so I had it decommissioned and told the council to use the funds elsewhere."

Alowen couldn't help but give Frazyk a soft look as they got in line. No wonder the man was mayor; he was so humble and thoughtful. He could demand to be separated from crowds and no one would think twice about it. As the line inched closer to the boarding gate, her heart beat faster. She could almost forget the Element Party; she was so excited about the orb. A small redheaded boy waved at her with his nose pressed to the glass as he took off in a bubble from the line next to theirs. Next to him, an older woman she presumed was his grandmother, was reading a magazine. Wolkenians were so lucky, Alowen decided. Traveling by electric orb seemed like no big deal to the lady.

"Ready?" Frazyk gave her a reassuring smile when they were up next.

"Ready as I'll ever be, I guess." Another orb floated down to loading height and a hatch slid open, revealing a circular couch.

"Milady." Frazyk waved her in. He chuckled at the blissful look on her face as warm air swept over them. "Our insulated glass makes the difference between roasting in summer and freezing in winter." They sat down, and he slid open a compartment under the couch to stash her bag while she fastened her seatbelt. Once enough people had filled up seating space, the hatch sealed, and the orb lifted into the air silently.

"Destination: Bachha." An electronic voice chimed.

"Huh." Alowen slumped back into her seat. "That's it?"

Maybe eagle riding had spoiled her. Traveling by orb seemed so much slower. No wonder that old lady was so immersed in her book.

Frazyk smirked. "Every tourist feels the same when they try an orb for the first time. It just needs half an hour to float out of the city. After that, well, put it this way, here is some cloud berry root. Chew it if you get nauseous." Alowen raised an eyebrow but pocketed the root.

"Alright."

She watched the city of Wolken slowly dwindle under its blanket of fog. The view was lulling her back to sleep. As the cityscape blurred to white, her eyes closed.

She opened them to find herself in an icy blue room with blank walls. The girl was back, but this time she sat stiffly in a tall chair draped with seaweed. Corals of greens and purples had grown into the chair. The woman, Jez, stood there too, looking meekly down at her hands.

"Do you understand?" An old man's cold voice came out of nowhere. Alowen almost jumped at how near he sounded. She looked around but somehow she couldn't turn all the way behind her. The girl nodded subduedly, and the voice went on. "You have your mother to thank. She insisted even us royalty aren't above tradition, otherwise, I'd have banned you from the opening and closing night processions. For banquets, Jez will take your place on the dais with the Bachhan royals."

This must be the king of Allurus. Alowen really wanted to get a good look at his face but seemed to be stuck in place. The girl barely moved. Her face was completely empty.

"You'll sit as you always have, poised and straight. You will not shame me or your mother any more than you already have. We don't need any more public embarrassments with that progressive fool, Sal, out there trying to corrupt our image. I trust you know what's at stake, daughter."

A jolt rocked Alowen awake. "Ahhh!"

"Whoa, easy there." Frazyk held up his hands. "You're alright, it's just the orb picking up speed now that we are out of Wolken."

Sure enough, the sky outside was now a bright blue. The cityscape had been replaced with mountains and birds that whizzed by, faster and faster.

"Are we really going three-hundred miles an hour right now? Alowen tried letting the astonishing view sweep away her latest vision. Just what on earth was happening in Al-lurus?

Frazyk was rambled on, oblivious to her spinning mind. "…well, hard to say these days. The engineer union claimed they can improve the orb's eagle-power, but so far we don't have any faster models released. Probably a good thing, it's a needless expenditure. I already promised the Alluran ambas-sador I'll take him for a Wolken tour after the Party in one of these. His entourage will love it."

Alowen blinked. "The Alluran ambassador? Sal?" What were the odds to hear him mentioned twice in a short peri-od?

Frazyk beamed. "Yes, very good. You remember even though he wasn't in your list! Well, turns out they are finish-ing their tour around Bachha's old cities with the Bachhan mayor when we arrive, so we'll meet him before we actually check in." He gave her one of his winks. "You'll see for yourself."

"I have so much to process." Alowen exhaled, watching the hills and clouds speed by.

It was somewhat calming, but her mind kept returning to the princess' new scene along with Frazyk's new informa-tion. Right, her program did cover this: a red-carpet proces-sion of the royals and Elemental leaders to start off the Party. So, the princess definitely was planned to appear in this public procession? It's no surprise the king of Earth's most conservative country was so strict on his daughter, even if it was disgusting. But it was just confusing after seeing her locked up so harshly the past few times. And if Jez was to replace her, what was the point? Alowen wanted to put her head in her hands. Instead, she put the cloud berry root in her mouth and chewed. Ugh! She almost spit it out from the initial stinging bitterness on her tongue.

Frazyk stifled a laugh. "I should have warned you. Not the most edible stuff, huh? Just wait, keep chewing."

She rolled her eyes but didn't spit it out yet. In a minute, the root softened and became sweet and mild.

Finally, Frazyk handed her a tissue. "You can go ahead and spit it out now. Don't swallow the root; it's too tough to digest."

"A warning would have been nice." She huffed.

Still, she did feel considerably calmer. Better ask for more later just in case. At least she would finally meet Sal for herself. Maybe then she could start filling in some blanks.

The orb floated for most of the afternoon. Alowen tried to relax and remember the names and questions she had practiced. Should she tell Frazyk about the vision and the previous ones? No, better not. This was no time for him to decide she was crazy. She wouldn't want him to feel like they made a mistake asking her to represent the Arbor. Better to try to process this dream later when she was alone. Now there were more important things to worry about.

When she still felt too tense to bring up her practice, she tried taking three deep breaths and pulling down her shoulders like Adenike taught her, which worked a bit. It helped when the orb landed at a couple of other stations so they could use the bathroom and buy some food. Thankfully, Frazyk seemed to sense she needed some space.

Around sunset, he pointed at the glass, "Look! A Bachha lift." Alowen shook herself and squinted at a tall mountain in the distance. At first, she frowned, trying to remember what a Bachha lift was. Then it hit her as the orb circled the volcano.

"It can't be!"

In the orange sunset, the craggy ledges looked pale and dry, like some rock monster's skin. It all cast a formidable appearance.

"Let's get ready." Frazyk opened the couch compartment.

The orb drifted into the volcano's mouth, where giant cups stuck out from the inner sides. As they neared, Alowen could see they were each bolted to a metal rail lining the volcano walls. As crimson-uniformed personnel watched from the rim, the orb lowered until it nestled securely into the cup, like an egg. Alowen couldn't keep her eyes off the whole thing. Her heart thumped furiously, just waiting for the cup to break and drop them down hundreds of feet.

"Hold on," Frazyk murmured.

Clamps locked the orb in place. Then the cup slid down the rail smoothly, passing a couple of other orbs on their way up. An electronic voice began telling the history of Bachha's volcano cities before they eventually moved to their underwater shell and converted the old volcanoes into giant lifts to connect their new domain to the world. The walls of the volcano were obsidian and so smooth they gave the impression they had been hand-polished. The jet-black walls were lit all the way down with soft pink flames that bounced like gentle waves.

Finally, the cup came to a stop at the bottom of a volcano, where the orb opened its hatch into a central hub.

"Smile, young scribe." Frazyk winked.

Outside, an Alluran girl waved a sign at them that read:

"Mayor Frazyk and Scribe Alowen." She wore a turquoise tunic that hit just above her knee, instead of the typical form-fitting Alluran garb which only covered private areas while remaining sleek and minimal for moving quickly through water.

"Mayor Frazyk, an honor to meet you!" the Alluran girl enthusiastically shook Frazyk's hand. "My name is Taman, one of Ambassador Sal's entourage. And this must be your guest and the Arbor scribe, Miss Alowen!"

"Hello, Taman! Thank you, we can't wait to meet your group." Frazyk's voice echoed through the room.

"I am honored to be here," Alowen added, smiling gently.

She tried not to stare at Taman's sharp canines as the girl smiled back brightly. "Yes, this way, come."

Taman led them out of the central hub into a grand hallway. The black walls of the volcano tunnel had suddenly transitioned into a beautiful jade green, and Alowen stared in awe. She fell behind a few steps and carefully touched the wall. It seemed to be a smooth, cool surface.

Surprisingly, the hallway wasn't as packed as Alowen expected. "Where's the crowd?"

"With the Party one day away, most of the traffic already made it into Bachha this past week," Taman explained. "They start making entry a little exclusive for the next few days. Over here..." She held open a glass door for them.

As they walked in, Water People left and right raised their heads or turned around. Frazyk shook hands with a broad grin while Alowen smiled and waved, shyer about receiving so much attention. Even with their friendliness, their fangs and thick muscles seemed so intimidating. They got to the center of a room where two men looked up from a board game, one a white-haired, ponytailed Bachhan in a dark red suit, and the other a dark-bearded Water person in a plain gray shirt and pants. This must be the mayor of Bachha and the Alluran ambassador. She started to greet them but stopped short when she saw a stocky young man next to them. Tousled curls had replaced the shaggy black hair she remembered from high school, and instead of the t-shirts he used to wear, he looked smartly fitted in a teal blazer.

Soren nodded at her. "Hello, Alowen."

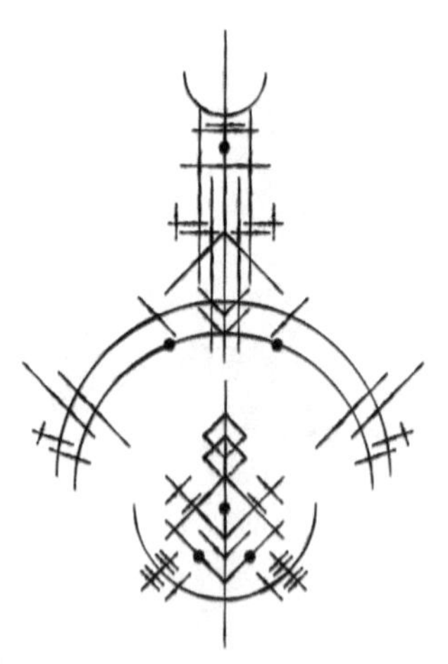

"Soren! What are you doing here? I had no idea you were going to be here."

Alowen hadn't seen him since he graduated school two years ago. She didn't even know he remembered her.

Soren only gave a modest shrug. "It's a long story. May I introduce you to Mayor Merrit and Ambassador Sal?"

Only then did Alowen register the gentlemen next to him watching her with a look of pleasant amusement. Frazyk looked surprised at her reaction to Soren. She had turned red, and a drop of sweat trickled down the back of her neck. She smiled feebly. "It's lovely to meet you; I've heard so much about you." Panic spread across her face when the words left her mouth. She hoped he wouldn't ask what she'd heard because her mind had gone completely blank.

Mayor Merrit gave her and Frazyk a quick, warm handshake—literally warm. Pink flames darted up and down his face. His eyes were hazel brown with just a tinge of pink. A papier mâché raven blinked at her intelligently on his shoulder. Rather than black, it was a patchwork of gold, copper, and silver.

Oh. She stared at the creature. Right, what was it Frazyk said about a Fire person's fire having an intelligence of its own? Still, this was the first time she had seen one of their papier mâché pets brought to life by their fire. What a beautiful thing.

"This time of year, it gets so hard to remember all the names and faces," he joked. "Not you, Frazyk. You've been around too often." Ambassador Sal's handshake was brief but solid. "You must be scribe Alowen, from the Arbor. Is this your first time visiting Bachha?"

His voice was the deepest she had ever heard, but anyone could hear his warm smile radiating through it. He didn't dress as regal as she imagined an Alluran official would, and with his short-cropped, lime-dark beard to finish off the look, he looked like any Arbor inner-city businessman.

"Yes sir, this is my first time here. I haven't seen much yet, but the jade hallway was quite beautiful." She leaned awkwardly to the side, wishing she had something more confident to say.

"That's right. All built by hand too." the ambassador waved a hand around the room. "It's the first time outside our country for some of my entourage, too. I haven't been to Bachha myself since my father brought me on a short work trip when he was ambassador. Thankfully, my right-hand man Soren here has been on enough trips around this region to be an extra guide. No offense to the mayor, but sometimes it just takes a local, ah, explanation."

The mayor and Frazyk laughed, and there were some chortles from Sal's entourage. Even Soren gave a small smirk. Alowen let herself breathe a little. Since when had Soren been traveling to Bachha?

Frazyk cleared his throat. "I must say, I've never seen so many Alluran youth outside your borders. Your king and governors must really like you."

The entourage around Sal shifted a bit on their feet. One man clenched his jaw, but when he saw Alowen looking, he flashed a smile.

"Ha that's funny." Sal pretended to look over his shoulder. "I've managed to bring some of our brightest teachers, dancers, singers, even scientists to the party. Though my king and governors wouldn't be happy to hear me say that word. They have been so kind in allowing me this little campaign already." He smiled, shrugging.

"Sal"—Soren checked a watch—"Maybe it's time to check into the Conche?"

"Ah, you're right." Sal cleared away the board game. "It's so easy to lose track of time. Alright, people, let's leave this suite as clean as it was before we came."

As his entourage tidied the room, he turned to Alowen and Frazyk. "Mayor Frazyk, Alowen, I'm so sad we won't be able to spend more time with you tonight after we check in, but it's been a long day for us, and we still have to unpack and rest."

Mayor Merrit chimed in. "But I am throwing a brunch tomorrow for any guest who would like to attend. Nice and informal. Will we see you there?"

The raven flapped its wings with excitement.

"Bright and early, too early, I am sure." Frazyk snorted and waved his long arm in mock protest.

Alowen bowed her head. "I'd be honored, Mayor Merrit. Thanks for inviting us."

"Oh, don't mention it, my dear," said the Mayor graciously. "Shall we?"

As the group picked up their luggage, he opened the door and strolled out first, followed by Sal.

"Frazyk! How have you been? Still flying around giving people neck cramps? Sal, I don't think you've heard the stories before, hm?"

Frazyk snorted as he and Alowen joined Mayor Merrit outside. "You old firefly. I see you haven't stopped exaggerating!"

The three men laughed as they walked down the hall. Alowen could only shuffle along behind them, half listening amusedly to their banter and half nervously eyeing the Water People who followed. Part of her wanted to make some new friends, but it honestly felt like going to a new school. Everyone already knew each other. And she had just flown in a glass ball from the mountains to the shore. Her neck and shoulders were stiff from sitting, and she was looking forward to some alone time this evening in her suite.

Thankfully, someone was here to make things easier for her. She looked up as Soren walked up next to her.

"I'm not surprised they picked you as the Arbor scribe," he said nonchalantly.

Alowen blinked. "Why's that?"

She had only been writing for the school magazine for a year when he graduated. There had been far more experienced columnists then.

"You had so much drive, even as a sophomore. You remember Purdy?"

She nodded. Purdy had been class president during Soren's year. She had also been editor-in-chief when Alowen started writing.

"Purdy said you were the best she had seen in a while." He looked at her sideways. "I wouldn't be surprised if she was on the Party organizing committee and picked you."

Alowen blushed. Purdy was one of the brightest and most hardworking students at her school. She had no idea the older girl thought of her that highly.

"If I really have her to thank for this opportunity, I'm going to give her the biggest hug—"

"She's a stay-at-home mother." Soren cut in.

"What?"

"It's true. Turns out her husband oversees one of Bachha's engineering labs where they manufacture spirit hookahs. You taste the wine in the fumes as you smoke. Not that we could visit the lab." He pursed his lips. "Our mayor controlled the itinerary."

"Purdy," Alowen muttered.

"Well, there's nothing much to it. I was surprised too when I saw her, but she said domestic life has actually been a much-needed escape from the career pressure she's faced most her life." He shrugged again. "And her husband earns enough, so she's comfortable. Works for those who can get married."

Alowen was silent for a minute. It was still a shock, everyone always assumed Purdy would rise high in many fields because she excelled everywhere— politics, economics, history, statistics. Who knew she would just throw it all away. The pressure made sense.

But when you are up and rising, you figure out quickly that love doesn't mix well with that. She sighed. Best not think about her own pressure now.

"So, Soren, what about you though?" She forced a smile and tried to focus on her curiosity. "How did you wind up here, working for…" She nodded at Sal.

"A few months after graduation I got a job in Wolken amongst the Element Liaison Federation. We tried to raise awareness about the lower welfare of mixed Element workers and lobbied for their rights." He shook his head. "My friend, Vino Masso, tried his best but he still wasn't President yet. We ran out of campaign funds, out of sponsors and advocates."

"What happened?" Alowen wished she had asked a little more about the Element Liaison Federation while she was at Wolken.

"We had to call off our campaigns and just get back to life. The Sky Council lost patience with us being on their streets, but Sal was visiting Wolken at the time. Vino told him about us, and when he knocked on my door all he asked was if I still want to help people." He sucked in a breath, and then kept on. "Ever since, we've been going around the world. The Arbor and Bachha and Allurus. We helped fundraise for Wolkenian cloud berry pickers, and we've tried to scout for mixed Element students like me, so we can offer them opportunities." He nodded toward his fellows around them.

Alowen thought about the way non-mixed students envied and isolated him at school. "It must have been difficult."

Soren's face looked bitter for a moment. "It was, yeah. I only found the Element Liaison Federation because nowhere else wanted to hire me. Some people didn't even want to admit they are mixed Elements."

There was so much Alowen didn't know about mixed Element struggles.

"Maybe this Party will help raise even more awareness for your cause?"

Soren shrugged. "Hopefully. If Sal's plan works, our activism can show the world we are not just a conservative, closed-off people, and that mixed Element people have a lot to contribute to society. Hold on, look!" He pointed. "We're reaching the tunnel that takes us under the sea."

Sure enough, dark blue light drew upon his face from ahead. They walked closer and Alowen clapped her hand over her mouth. Walking underwater was beautiful. The city couldn't be too far down because she could already see glaring spotlights waving around from under the tunnel. They highlighted schools of fish all around the tunnel and even some squid.

An enormous fish with shimmering rainbow scales moved in, its eyes large and expressive as it swooped close to the glass where it paused. Chills crawled down her spine at the eye contact. As it turned slowly, her breath paused at the bright coral behind it. She never knew how tall and intricate coral structures were, jutting out along the sand like a miniature city.

Frazyk turned and mouthed, *Oh. My. Cosmos.* at Alowen. She nodded enthusiastically. It hit her then how she was the only person in that group to not have gone under the sea before, and she appreciated Frazyk even more for being excited along with her. She tried not to look at Soren, but it was hard when she was trying to look around.

Finally, she felt his tap on her shoulder. "Step carefully. The floor."

Several feet ahead the tunnel sloped downward, though small bumps on the tile helped her shoes find grip.

"Not far now," Mayor Merrit called.

Ten minutes later, warm lights gave the inside of the tunnel an orange glow. They were definitely close now.

"Finally," Alowen murmured. She had welcomed the chance to stretch her legs, after the long day in the orb, but the walk was starting to ache her feet. They were definitely close now.

Soren must've heard because he said, "Grand terminal's right there."

"Oh, the terminal. We're so close!" one of the Water People said excitedly.

In fact, all of Sal's entourage looked delighted. Only Soren kept a stoic face, cool everywhere he went. Her irritation didn't last long under her own curiosity. She was this close now to Bachha.

Just then, Alowen stepped out of the glass tunnel and her dark blue surroundings. Before her sprawled a cavernous chamber, gleaming white and dark gold everywhere she looked. Giant bronze bowls hung from the ceiling on chains, each burning with amber and jade flames. Ports lined the walls where electric orbs rested, leaning against hatches.

"I didn't know orbs go underwater too," she said in wonder.

"Oh, these aren't Wolkenian orbs. We have Alluran orbs, but they aren't here." Merrit turned. "Bachha uses bubble pods to float tourists up to catch sunrises when the sea is calm. Some nights, engineers need them to check out Bachha's shell." He caught her look and laughed. "Don't worry, our city has held up underwater for decades from cloud crystals and its reinforced design. Even the portals we set up to let in Alluran orbs can't compromise its structuresmerr and that's complicated tech. But—*But*—tomorrow"—he shook his finger in the air—"tomorrow, Frazyk'll take you in his bubble pod up to my morning patio."

Frazyk winked at her. "Technically, Bachha reserves one for me every visit. I'll take you back here tomorrow. But come, the Conche awaits."

They left the chamber into a foyer, empty except for a few uniformed sentries who smiled, bowing at the company. From the ceiling protruded a pillar displaying four massive clocks, one for each region. Below it, a brass fountain towered twice the height of Frazyk. It looked like a three-tiered goblet spouting clear water. Its sides were engraved with seagulls, volcanoes, and men holding fire. Merrit placed his palm proudly against it.

"This has never stopped flowing with freshwater since our most famous sculptors and magicians built it centuries ago."

Further, the foyer opened to a starry night. Alowen frowned. *Stars under the sea?* She followed Frazyk and Merrit out to the entrance and gasped at the expanse of magnificence. From here, Bachha looked like a bowl of diamonds under a glittery, purple sky. A spiraling highway miles and miles wide looped around malls, domed hotels, and even lakes with fountains spurting jets of multicolored steam, winding upward endlessly.

Merrit happily escorted them down the terminal steps where four vehicles waited. They were some sort of exquisitely crafted close-roofed chariots, with silver-plated sides lined with white fairy lights. Smiling footmen waved Alowen into the lead chariot with Merrit, Frazyk, and Sal. Soren saw the Alluran entourage into the other chariots and then entered the second one. She barely noticed it all; things were moving so fast.

Soft rosy flames licked at his ashy-gray skin and emphasized his beaming smile. The man was proud of his city. By the time their rumbling pace slowed, Alowen had to blink a few times.

Frazyk squeezed her shoulder lightly. "We'll have some food and rest soon. Promise." He glanced past her out the window. "Here we are! Pulling into the Conche entrance!"

Alowen's stomach lurched again. Here we go, no more time to prepare. She clutched her satchel tightly. All she had to do was smile, breathe, and be herself. More valets opened their chariots and welcomed them onto a pearly pink sidewalk. As they addressed the leaders, no one noticed her for a moment, and she stared around, mouth falling open.

Torches of pink and purple flames lined the streets and corridors, sending a soft light ricocheting off the surfaces. Various ornate glass sculptures stood about the courtyard while Water cascaded down the walls into beautiful pools where fire danced off the surface of the water. The fire in Bachha was unusual, true, but how could it stay lit while in contact with water? Never mind, it seemed wasteful to her to analyze all the beauty.

"Young miss?" Frazyk called down from a flight of gilded stairs at the Conche's entrance. "These strong, young men have our bags. Let's go."

A shiver of excitement went up her spine as a well-dressed bellhop extended his hand to help her up the steps.

"Miss?"

No one's ever treated her with so much class, even at Sielo. She smiled, taking his hand. Moments later, they were ushered through the lobby amongst scattered, glowing blue holograms of people. Mechanical songbirds perched on golden and silver branches sticking from the circular walls, filling the air with flute and harp melodies. So, it wasn't an old wives' tale—a fire person's flames could animate various objects: dolls, paintings, maybe even statues. It was a struggle not to keep turning as she followed her guide to the receptionist counter. The lady did a double-take as the group drew close. Even the papier-mâché cat on her counter stopped playing with its ball of yarn.

"Mayor Merrit! What a pleasure!" She looked over the group and clicked her pen. "Ah, Mayor Frazyk and Ambassador Sal, too! We have reservations for you and these lovely ladies and gentlemen."

"Let's take a look. Lovely." Frazyk hovered over the counter.

Alowen wandered over to one of the holograms as they talked. It looked like a woman in a chef's hat holding a basket of bread.

"Welcome to Bachha and the Conche! I'm Selma, and right now you're standing in the southwest corner of the lobby. Did you know, southwest Bachha was the district where bakers from the Arbor set up their business? They were the region's first imports for its new underwater location."

"You learn lots of new things that way," said someone as holographic Selma droned on. Alowen turned to see a Wolkenian girl in a floral pink dress. She looked like an elf with birds singing over her. "Bachhans love learning, it's part of their adventurous spirit." She put her hand out. "Scribe Iris. I take it you are Scribe Alowen?"

"Oh!" Alowen had completely forgotten about the other scribes. She shook hands.

"Have you been here the past few days?" Iris smiled. Her lipstick was bright pink too. "Straight from Astara. I thought it would be helpful to get familiar with Bachha, find out everyone's favorite party spots. It's too bad you just got here, but I can tell you if you want."

Alowen raised her eyebrows. Some of the guests were well over nightlife age, but she didn't want to be rude. "We probably don't have enough time right now, but tomorrow I'm going to a brunch Mayor Merrit's hosting. It sounds fun, I can't wait to eat free food and meet guests." Her belly growled, and she blushed. Oops, hopefully, Iris didn't hear that.

"Oh yes, the brunch." Iris waved lazily. "Here's a tip. Almost everyone sleeps in tomorrow morning; they need their energy for the Party. If it's free food you want, tomorrow morning I'll take you out to this gorgeous ziti palace with an authentic fire oven. They even crisp fries from Arbor potatoes with battered lobster. I'll pay."

"Alowen?" Frazyk walked up. "Oh, hello, Iris. I didn't see you there. How's Bachha been?"

"Oh, but the night's too young, Mayor. I'll have to tell you another time. My research awaits." Iris curtsied and turned on the spot.

Frazyk turned back to Alowen, sighing. "I say Astara's a bit too intense. Our people end up letting loose so much here."

"I can understand." Nightlife may not be Alowen's style, but she had endured enough stress she wouldn't judge. "Well, shall we head on up?" Frazyk held up two key cards. "They are bringing our things to the rooms now. And then you can order some room service. Sal, Merrit, it's been a long day; we'll see you tomorrow."

Alowen nodded. Her stomach was killing her.

Even the curved elevator was lavish, with swirls of platinum along the pale green glass walls. How could the hotel afford to maintain this? Not one fingerprint, they must have had someone polishing everything on the hour! A whole team of people, really. She glanced at the elevator numbers and did a double take, were they already at the fourth floor in half a minute? This thing moved *fast*.

"See that?" Frazyk pointed out the green glass at a magnificent palace on a hill.

"Is that…?"

"That, my dear, is the Bachhan Palace. The royal family lives there."

She hadn't seen many pictures, but none showed its full dimensions. Here, it was absolutely enormous even from a distance—practically three interlocking palaces. She couldn't even fathom what it looked like on the inside.

"We'll party there tomorrow." Frazyk clapped her on the shoulder. Just then, the elevator opened on the sixth floor. "Alright, my back is dead. I need food and sleep."

Adenike was right, everything was purple. Most of the hues were light enough to be more a purplish cream, but here and there were bolder accents. When they reached the rooms, Frazyk winked goodnight and shut his door.

Alowen's breath caught as she opened hers. The entire wall behind her enormous platform bed was a mirror. A blue glass chandelier hung from the ten-foot ceiling. The centerpiece was a swirl of turquoise ocean waves, trailing down strings of blue jewels, each with a mermaid at the end of it. The bedspread was covered in long white feathers, impractical yet beautiful. She stepped in and turned slowly. This room was so large it could swallow her whole.

"Good evening, and welcome to Bachha!"

"Who's there?" Alowen whirled, raising her fists instinctively. Uncle Rogan had given her some lessons on how and where to punch. But it turned out to be another hologram from the corner of her room. This one looked like a young, attractive fire woman in a valet suit.

The hologram continued. "The city that makes its own sunlight. Please know that I am equipped with the full history records of this city, at your disposal at any point of your visit. For a complete list of scheduled performances and attractions this evening, press one on your touchpad."

A digital touchpad materialized.

"For room service, press two. To deactivate me, press nine. To re-materialize me and browse the options, press zero. I am happy to help you with sightseeing and restaurant recommendations as well! Enjoy your stay." The hologram became silent but stayed where it was.

Alowen wandered over to the bed and brushed her fingers over it. Impossibly, the bed here was even softer than the one at Frazyk's. She nearly lay on it for a moment but held off for now. If she lay down, she might not wake till the sun was high. Alright, first things first— food.

She turned back to the touchpad. Right, two for room service. Tapping two gave her a whole range of options, from being able to call a staff member, to browsing the menu on her own. She picked the latter, and the number of dishes it provided her was stunning. They could get all this underwater? Even chicken and beef?

She ended up choosing the chicken sandwich and a cloudberry juice. Guess she really missed Wolken. Barely a couple minutes later, Alowen opened her door to a knock and eagerly accepted her order from a Conche staff. She was about to close the door when he stopped her politely.

"Excuse me, miss. This letter is for you."

Frowning, she put her food onto a dresser and took the envelope he held out to her. "Uh…" But when she looked at the handwriting, a deep breath gushed out of her. "Thank you."

"Good evening, miss." The hotel keeper bowed slightly and left.

Alowen closed the door and sat at the foot of her bed in a trance. Here was the first letter from her mother in days. She slid it open.

Dear Alowen,

Uncle Rogan said you would be in Bachha by now, so he had me address it here instead of Mayor Frazyk's house. Was Wolken as grand as they say? Do you miss the food at home? Don't you dare say you don't!

I hope you've made a friend or two. I know you tend to keep to yourself a bit when you get uncomfortable, but I do hope you have people to confide in about all your experiences. They are so BIG, Alowen. You must feel like your eyes have been opened to the vastness of the world. I can't tell you how proud I am of all your accomplishments. Listen, this is only the beginning. You've been such a detective ever since you were a little girl. Do you remember when you hid around the corner and heard Uncle Rogan and I whispering about your pet chicken that had passed? You were so stoic when you confronted us. You came into this world with a bold soul. The second you were born, you always had your father's passion and determination. I can't tell you how proud I am of all your accomplishments; he would be too, I promise.

But growing up is hard, yes. Maturing is a long process. Even your uncle and I work on it for the rest of our lives! You've always been so excited to get to the "finished result," but when it comes to becoming the best version of you, you will never be finished. I wish you could see through my eyes how much you've grown, how quickly. You've got this, Alowen. You are going to do so well in Bachha.

Just please promise me you will take care of yourself. You are the most important person in my life, and I need to know you've eaten three square meals each day! I miss you terribly and I do hope you will come home and rest for a bit once the commotion is over. I can't wait to hear all the incredible experiences you must be having. Write soon, please.

Love, Mom

Alowen hugged the letter to her chest. Her eyes swelling with tears as she took a seat on the edge of the bed. It was so good to read her mom's words. She would write to her mother soon, but not tonight. She ate her food in big, hurried bites and brushed her teeth before she changed into night clothes, her eyelids growing heavier with each moment. Sleep swooped in the moment she lay down.

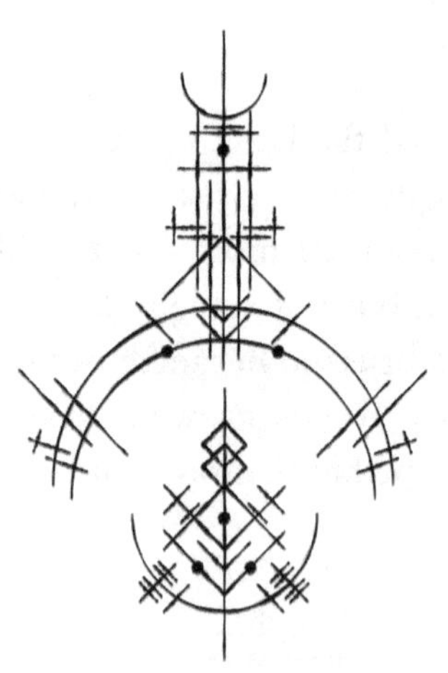

Alowen opened her eyes to see the chandelier above, the room feeling like a huge, blue fishbowl around her. So dreamy. She rolled onto her side, burrowing her head deeper into the pillow. Yesterday felt so—had she really gone down a volcano and walked through the sea in a tunnel?

"Alowen."

Mmm?

"Alowen?"

Ughh. It was Frazyk at the door. She rolled over and covered her head with a pillow. No one should have to function until at least two days after long-distance travel. Make it stop.

"Earth to Alowen. Miss, brunch is in an hour. You may want to get yourself cleaned up. The terminal staff are already warming my bubble."

She could just see his annoying wink now. Groaning, she dragged herself up and trudged to the vanity. Alright, one thing at a time. Brunch first, then party tonight.

***

The Grand Terminal seemed to loom even higher in the daytime. Maybe it was the number of people shuffling through and making it seem larger in comparison. It was just as packed here as the streets. People bustled everywhere in the most exaggerated outfits she had ever seen. A woman's red dress swished along the floor as six men followed her and scattered white rose petals behind her. They swept past a young boy on a small platform in some type of reflective, silver suit juggling six stuffed toys.

Bachha wasn't like Wolken, she realized. Where people stopped to greet Frazyk, no one here batted an eye at the Wolkenian mayor among them. Maybe the city's grown normalized to celebrities.

Frazyk strode toward one of the bubble ports against the wall. "This time, Merrit's given me Bubble Two. Right here."

A sentry slid open the bubble hatch, and Alowen followed Frazyk into the pod. She grunted and slouched into a seat in front of the coffee machine. Frazyk waited for her to fill up her mug before he pressed a button on a machine that looked like a cash register.

"All aboard."

The pod doors closed, and the bubble disengaged from its port, floating up through the water as though the shell expelled it. She took a deep breath and sipped coffee as she watched the water turn lighter. A stingray glided into view alongside them, with slow, rhythmic flaps of its fins. A school of bright-orange fish darted away from the bubble, shooting behind a mushroom-like coral patch. *Relax. Be yourself.* Frazyk kept doing his crossword, humming under his breath, which strangely helped.

Gradually, more sunbeams lightened the water around them, their bubble rising under open sky, and bobbing on slow waves. Some yards away there seemed to be a wide platform floating on the surface…with furniture on it. Alowen squinted through the glass.

"Hold on." Frazyk fiddled with the control console. "Bachha used to hire Sky People to control their bubble pods, but those would roll and all the passengers would get thrown about." He chuckled, Alowen staring at him incredulously. "I know, I'm horrible for laughing. But—ah, here." He twisted a knob and pressed another button. The bubble slid forward and smoothly through the calm sea. "Finally, some Bachhan engineers attached propellers to the bottom of a pod, and here we are."

As they pulled near the floating platform, Alowen could see three sections to it: a seating area of round tables and curved leather chairs, chrome dishes in a long array, and a wide pier extending outward at least six feet. That had to be the best place to catch a view.

Frazyk stood up, licking his lips. "I hope they have poached ash-goose eggs. I am starving!"

Alowen didn't feel much like eating, but she couldn't wait to see what else Bachha had on its menu. Goodbye to cloud berries for now. She drained her mug and stood near the pod hatch with him.

As the bubble reached the patio, a Bachhan attendant was already waiting with a papier mâché tortoise next to him. Its shell glowed molten orange like lava.

"Good morning, Mayor Frazyk and Scribe Alowen. Welcome to Mayor Merrit's brunch. Today is a sunny morning with safe winds and low tides. Sit anywhere you like and choose anything from the buffet."

He waved to an array of chrome dishes lining a concave wall where more stewards waited. There had to be at least twenty dishes; Bachhans clearly didn't play when it came to their breakfast. She would have to start slow and simple if she didn't want to get full too quickly.

"Hoho, don't mind if I do." Frazyk almost skipped over.

Alowen couldn't see other guests. Even Wombat was

missing. But as she loaded her plate, something flashed in the distance. Another bubble! It surfaced and glided over. When it opened, a Wolkenian lady in a sunhat and green frock stepped out gracefully, followed by an overweight, grey-haired Bachhan man in glasses, beach shorts, and a t-shirt that boomed "Life of the Party" in yellow blocks. Shading his eyes, he waved away the attendant and stumbled after his companion toward the buffet. Alowen eyed them curiously, rooting around her memory. This had to be…

"Can we help?" They both watched her, the lady with a confused smile, while the man's eyebrow was raised.

Alowen stepped back, blushing. "I am so sorry. I didn't mean to stare. Just—"

"Wanted an autograph, it figures." The man sighed and kept scooping up honey oatmeal. "You see, Orchid? Gain seventy pounds, powder your hair, move away to a lake cabin, and still, everyone wants Dexran's signature."

"*You're* Dexran?" Alowen nearly dropped her plate. The last time she had seen him on a pixilator, he looked…well, the opposite of this. "And you must be Orchid, the Bluehils folk singer?"

"Last I checked." The author shot her a smug look as he spooned tuna and corn onto a flatbread.

"Dexran, it's too early for this. She's one of the new scribes," Orchid scolded. She looked a bit younger than Alowen's mother, but her voice rasped like a fifty-year-old smoker. "Pay him no attention, Miss. His books are bad enough."

Dexran placed a coconut on his tray and blew her a kiss. "Still sells better than your albums."

Orchid rolled her eyes and then smiled at Alowen. "Will you join us? Your food will get cold soon, and then Dexran'll have to eat two brunches."

With a glance at Frazyk, Alowen awkwardly followed the

pair to a table, but he was happily talking to a couple of stewards over his eggs. Spending time with the guests was exactly what she was supposed to do. Frazyk would be fine.

Maybe she should at least turn on her tape recorder. Thankfully, they were paying their brunch more attention than her, so they didn't spot her doing it. That would have been awkward. Orchid happened to glance over. Alowen quickly shoved her hand with the recorder under the table and took a demonstrative bite.

"WOW, these potatoes are incredible. Did the cook these in bacon fat?"

Dexran pointed at her a little too enthusiastically. "A woman with TASTE! When I cook, I ONLY use bacon fat. Vegetables, meat, rice, you name it. Come to think of it, one time I poured bacon fat on my ice cream; I have to say it wasn't bad."

"Write a book on that sometime, why don't you?" Alowen didn't mean to snark, but Dexran's carefree, slobby attitude brought it out.

He slapped his knee and snorted with his mouth full. "Oh, I like you! You are not like the other scribes we met before. 'Blah blah blah' books. 'Blah blah blah' writing. Get a life already. At least you have some personality."

"Have you ever thought about it? Not writing?" Alowen tasted some tomatoes. They were picked just this morning, judging by the juicy crunch.

"Oh, sure. Lately, I've been learning to weave blankets out of oversized yarn. It's very physical. You have to use your whole body. Some of them have turned out pretty well, actually. I get sick of sitting all hunched over writing all the time." Dexran finished his flatbread and started spooning chunks from his coconut. "You want an interview? Tell your readers all that. I live. I observe. I learn. I enjoy."

"Dexran, the world-class author, you couldn't come up

with a more eloquent quote than that?" Orchid took a sip of her coffee.

"Still more eloquent than the songwriters who wrote your songs."

Alowen watched them bicker. Beneath the jabs and snipes, they seemed like refreshingly close friends who spoke their minds and clearly knew how to appreciate life to its fullest.

"What do you regret?" she asked quietly.

A shadow covered their table from clouds shifting over the sun. She shivered.

"Too many things, girl." He wasn't eating anymore. "Too many things. But when it's my time. I can go knowing I've given every situation all I can give. Like that Water Dragons Legends book."

Alowen paused. "I'm sorry?"

But Dexran ranted on with Orchid patting his back. "They had such a beautiful tale, and all I wanted to do was show it. I was willing to credit the storytellers, the archivists, the indigenous elders. Most of the profits would go to them, I was okay with that." He wiped his mouth. "They pulled back the book after ten copies. And they definitely did not want their prophecy out there."

Alowen hadn't heard this part. "And…why not?"

"Who knows?" Orchid slid in as Dexran went back to his coconut. "Perhaps they didn't want to support the idea of the elements merging."

"Stupid, close-minded fishheads," Dexran muttered.

Alowen's mind was searching. What were the details again? "It's an old prophecy, though. Maybe they just didn't want fresh publicity?"

"Old, fresh, who cares; they're fishheads," Dexran slurped out the last of his coconut with a straw, then pointed at the sky. "Orchid, look, an ash goose!" Alowen looked up in time to catch a dark, slim shape sweep overhead. It faded in and out of fluffy clouds until it disappeared over the Bachha's Lift with an ending bright red flash.

"Beautiful, no?" Orchid looked wistful. "Especially that scarlet tail. When they were wild flocks, they were like one giant black arrow in formation."

Alowen imagined ash geese soaring en masse over the sea and volcanoes, the way Arbor ones passed over her home every Fall. "Are they endangered?"

"Far from it," said a new voice cheerily.

It was a young Bachhan man who looked subtly familiar. Sal and Soren stood next to him with some of their people. This time, all the Water People wore their traditional swimwear. Their wiry, coral-green bodies firm as rock. Alowen took one glance and tried not to stare. Behind them, several others of Sal's entourage were tucking into their brunch. The young Bachhan lifted a plate with a giant omelet crusted with parsley and mushroom.

"We've bred their numbers to an all-time high. Demand for goose eggs is against the roof, and we have more than enough to ship mail and goods around the world. What else do you do with long-distance birds?"

Dexran rolled his eyes and got up to stomp back to the buffet. Orchid followed with a sharp look at the man.

"Not very popular with those two." He chuckled.

"My king would've agreed with them." Sal said, sipping from a glass. "More shipping and commerce than in his day."

"Too much extravagance for him, yes." The man smiled, "It's a shame. There's so much to reap from the other regions. Maybe after the Party we can sit down with him to discuss some...advancements."

"Come, Leiland. I don't want to give him a bad report."

But the man only grinned and stooped to shake Alowen's hand. "Sorry, I don't mean to be rude. I am Leiland,

Mayor Merritt's son. My father couldn't make it last minute, so here I am."

So that's why he looked so familiar. The man even had his father's ponytail and pink-brown eyes. Suddenly one of her visions flooded back.

Lei's finishing his plans, said Jez as she knelt before the princess. *Are you that Lei?* How…unexpected.

"Good to see you, Leiland." She shook his hand. "Please thank your father for setting this up for us."

Leiland toasted her. "You must be scribe Alowen from the Arbor. Yes, we are often tied up with work, so he's really sorry he couldn't be around. As for me, I'm looking forward to spending time with normal people for a change."

The son was as jolly as his father, it seemed. *Give trust to get trust. If you tell your secrets, you will hear many of theirs.*

"I don't know what it's like being a mayor's son, but I'm already so busy as a student; it must be terribly hard to relax in your position." Alowen looked at Soren. "But you've been a student and you're dabbling in politics."

Everyone made sympathetic noises.

"It's a tough world," he admitted. "But at least these functions have killer food."

"He's right." Leiland nodded to the buffet. "All my life, I never understood why all these celebrities pass up free foreign delicacies. More raw tuna and clams for me."

Alowen looked around, stunned. Iris did warn her, but aside from Dexran, Orchid, and the Water People there were only two other guests on the patio. Did these people really take a function like this so lightly?

"Must be a rich person thing."

"And that's the real reason we are trying to build better relations with the rest of the world." Sal smacked his palm with his fist. "We share their food, then we share their wealth."

Everyone laughed. Even Soren smiled. It hit Alowen then how she was surrounded by tall Allurans with fangs and thick muscles, but she felt safe. Somehow, she had made friends.

"Well"—she glanced over at the two new guests, slinging her satchel back on—"I have a job to do and friends to make."

"Hold on, Alowen." Leiland put down his glass. "I'll join you on my way for more pineapple. More for us, so we might as well not waste it."

"Oh, I'll try some. We don't have those in the Arbor. Too cold." She glanced his way as they walked back to the buffet.

What did this friendly man have to do with the weak, scared Alluran princess?

"Have you grown up there your whole life?" Leiland piled his plate with slices of pineapple. She nodded and he went on. "Here's a tip from a local. Bachha can be overwhelming, especially before the Element Party." He looked around at the idyllic patio, the pleasant and ever helpful stewards, the sunny sky, and the calm tides, dropping his voice dramatically. "Don't let it get to you."

She laughed at the ironic contrast. "Did an Alluran conservative tell you to say that?"

He bit into his pineapple, shaking his head. "A land demon's pit is the nicest of their comments about Bachha. Just between you and me, that's why only progressives are here."

None of this would make it onto her article. "And does your father feel the same way as you?"

"Well, I…hm." He paused and swallowed with a shudder. "Ooh, my sweet tooth is too bad, I shouldn't. Well, he wouldn't say any of this, but the truth is, if Allurus had half our innovative minds, our openness to new ideas, our tolerance, it would be so much more…"

He sighed, taking another bite. "The sweetness is so bad for me, but so good. But I guess I can see Bachha's darker sides. Not everyone is as nice as they seem. People will try directing your interviews for their benefit. And if they don't like your drafts, you can expect lots of money, or other offers."

She thought about Dexran and Orchid. "It looks like I've gotten lucky so far with my interviews."

"They can't do more than that." Leiland dabbed his lips. "But like I said, don't let it get to you. The best scribes don't give into that pressure and still write the truth. I have that feeling about you."

She looked over to her right, where Dexran was telling a story to some of the Water People. She had made it this far.

She turned back to Leiland. "Don't worry, my next story will be: 'Bachhan mayor's son bashes Elemental Party guests.'"

Leiland laughed, walking away. "You'll do just fine here, Alowen. Just fine."

She did just that for the next hour. The two latest guests turned out to be Seema, a well-known flute player, and Grym, a classical sonnet poet. By the time she turned off her tape recorder and went back to Frazyk's bubble, she had some idea for their stories.

"Someone had fun," Frazyk commented. He looked her up and down. "Who's this confident young lady?"

She sighed as she sat. "It's a very tired young lady now." The sun was higher now and more waves rolled over the sea. "We have seven hours before the Party, right?"

"Mm…better take advantage of it." Frazyk rubbed an eye. He looked exhausted. "I'm sleeping off my food coma, and then I must prep this face for the Procession."

She'd almost forgotten. Thank the cosmos she wouldn't be needed for that. Wait—the princess would be there. She sat frozen while the bubble lowered under the water. This very evening, she would finally see the girl from her visions.

Remembering the princess brought back her conversation with Leiland. The mayor's son seemed friendly and caring, even funny. But she couldn't forget what she heard. *Lei's finishing his plans.* Under that warm persona, Leiland had something brewing—good or bad, she didn't know.

When they got back, Alowen promised to meet Frazyk in the Conche lobby before they left for the Party together. She locked her door before collapsing on her bed. A function like that wouldn't normally tire her out, but puzzling over the mystery of Leiland turned out to be really draining.

***

"One last time?"

She twirled on the spot again. The dress had stayed as pristine as its first presentation.

"Come here." Leena held up a brush. With a few dabs she touched up Alowen's blush and then stepped back. "Aaaand you're officially ready."

Alowen barely recognized her own reflection. At Frazyk's place, she looked like a young woman, not a teenager. Here Leena had transformed her into a swan, a princess. Her hair was perfectly curled into shining black waves. Her eye makeup was smokey, mysterious, and she had a hint of deep red on her lips.

She could only shake her head. "I'm speechless."

"Good." Leena blew her a kiss, even as she packed her things one-handed. "You'll need your words for the Party. I'll see you there?"

Alowen nodded. "You have other guests to take care of?"

"I have a team with almost every celebrity right now."

Leena headed for the door. "But some are…emergency cas-es." Alowen laughed. "Good luck."

"I'll need it more than you."

The door closed. Alowen eyed the clock. She had to be going soon, too, if she wanted to get down to the foyer with Frazyk on time. He had his Procession to join, and the roads were probably packed already.

A few minutes later, she found him in the foyer checking his nails.

"Frazyk! You look like you could own the world."

He wore a blood red suit with a metallic black shirt peeking through. A metallic black top hat with a matching red ribbon around the base sitting neatly on his head. To her surprise, he had a quill pin on his lapel like hers.

He tapped it, smiling. "Got to support our scribes, yes?"

She smiled warmly. "Thanks, that's really sweet of you."

"Well, let's get going! We don't want to miss anything."

They stepped out of the building and onto the street where a shining carriage awaited. It looked like a horizontal light blue pear with large white, silver spoked wheels.

"Madam." Frazyk bowed, opening the door for her.

She carefully moved in, onto a luxurious deep blue velvet seat, and smoothed her dress out. There was no driver in front of them, just a brightly lit panel with a map and a search bar.

"How does this thing work?" she worried aloud as Frazyk hopped in next to her. "Oh. it's simple. These carriages are powered with fire the same way as the other objects around Bachha. We just select the Bachhan Palace like this"—he popped a spindly finger onto the map—"and away we go!"

The carriage rolled swiftly up the streets. The sun was just starting to set but already crowds of people were cheerfully dancing, drinking, mingling, and eating street food on the sidewalks. They passed the odd pair of small stages where bands or solo musicians jammed out, surrounded by throngs of people wearing vibrant costumes. A shiver of excitement ran up Alowen's spine as the electric mood in the streets passed through to her. There was so much to see, she could barely register the turns they were making.

Finally, the carriage slowed to a stop behind another carriage along the sidewalk, and she got her first closeup look at the Bacchan Palace. The thing was practically a fortress, built a grand seventy foot tall. Across the road from it, a cordon of guards held back eager paparazzi. That relieved her some. She wasn't spending her night mobbed by people less gracious with their questions delivery.

The carriage in front of them pulled ahead a few feet, and they followed. There were more up front, letting guests out into the entrance. Finally, it was their turn, and the carriage door opened on its own. Frazyk hurried around, extending an arm.

"Watch your step."

She held her dress up a bit as she stepped out but then stopped short with a gasp. Really, Bachhans never did things half measure! Forty-foot-high doors stood open at the top of a flight of stairs, flanked by two ruby lion statues. Torches mounted along the walls on either side of the door cast a glow on them, and the fire reflections seemed to dance across the lions' bodies. The Bachhan Palace couldn't be more domineering in stature and décor.

"We got to move; the next carriage is waiting." Frazyk linked his arm through hers and led her up the palace steps toward the doors, through its foyer. She stared about at the busts of past monarchs that had reigned from this palace until Bachha ceded power to mayoral offices instead. Tall windows of stained glass flickered all sorts of colors by candlelight. Unfortunately, she didn't get to take in the whole magnificent foyer before Frazyk reached the Banquet Hall entrance where two gentlemen waited checking people off a list. Violin and flutes warbled through the doors with each admission.

Finally, the doormen smiled up as Frazyk and Alowen approached. "Mayor Frazyk, yes sir. And Scribe Alowen. Come on in." They pulled apart the doors, and the pair of them stepped onto a scarlet carpet embroidered with golden silk dragons that ran the length of the Banquet Hall. She almost tripped over herself staring at it. Thankfully, no one saw that. Amidst the music, there was a low hum of hundreds of voices, talking and laughing. Wait staff in glittering black suits and dresses offered appetizers at each table. Candles hovered on top of silver dishes as high as Frazyk's head. But he weaved in and out among the harmless Bacchan fire, past tables full of well-dressed elites.

"Investors, company chairmen, record producers…" Frazyk whispered, pausing here and there to grin and wave. "Alright, your table is—"

"Here," a voice cut in.

They turned to see Soren sitting nearby at a table with only three empty seats left. Around him were a few more elites, most of them paying attention elsewhere. Alowen's eyes fell on a card with her name.

"Where are you sitting?" She turned to Frazyk.

"Up there." Frazyk nodded up at an elaborate dais where a long table in cream cloth lay waiting. He shrugged at her apologetically. "Duty calls, I'm afraid."

"That's okay." She gestured to Soren. "I have an old friend here."

Frazyk accepted a slim flute of wine from a waiter and toasted her. "Have fun then. I'll see you later."

Soren shifted to face her as she sat. "You look nice."

"Thanks, friend. You've cleaned up too." He was wearing a lush green tux with the swirl of grape-purple waves along his cuffs and lapel. A golden seahorse brooch sat on his breast.

"Where is Sal, where's the rest of your crew?"

"Scattered around." He waved around the hall. "Here to tell anyone who's interested about us, what we do, what we hope to accomplish for Allurus. Together, maybe we can create some outsider interest in helping our element overturn its conservative policies."

Before Alowen could think about that, a waiter glided in with a plate of figs wrapped in ham. "Would you like one, miss?" Alowen hadn't realized how hungry she was until she snuck the delicacy into her mouth. She just about sighed at the sweetness of the fig and the salt of the ham.

"That good, huh?" said a Bachhan man on her other side.

She blushed and dabbed her mouth with a napkin, chewing quickly. "I'm sorry, sir. I just—"

"Aww, you're alright. This food is sheer ecstasy, no one can deny that," said the gentleman amiably. He reached out to shake Alowen's and then Soren's hand. "I'm Bennai Rosseur; this is my wife Lita." A heavyset woman next to him waved casually before turning back to her conservation.

Alowen caught snatches of the words "funds" and "interests," so the Wolkenian she was talking to had to be some banker.

"We are property investors, and we've just come back from a vacation in the Arbor. This is a nice homecoming, no?" He chuckled over his wine.

"Oh, the Arbor!" Alowen exchanged quick looks with Soren. "That's where we're from! We've—we've lived there most of our lives. Where did you vacation?"

"The Cherry Trout Falls out west." Mr. Rosseur said with some satisfaction. "Two months, three weeks in the village of Oreyal. The locals were so hospitable, we couldn't just leave too soon."

"How nice." Soren said slowly. Mr. Rosseur beamed at him.

"Isn't it? Anyways, we were thinking of buying some land up there and leasing it out. We can't miss out on that kind of rustic opportunity around here. It's so"—he smacked his lips—"quaint."

Blood rushed to Alowen's face. The four elements had agreed for years that there was still unexplored land out there. Any expansion should happen there first. Before she could say anything, the lights dimmed abruptly, and the buzz in the room fell silent. Everyone stared at the entryway for a few long moments. Then the candles flared up, switching from pink to dark blue as an Alluran choir walked in filling the air with flutelike voices. Ten people, twenty, thirty, all sounding like waves pulling in slowly upshore. It was probably one of the older Alluran dialects, back soon after the Frozen Years. Next came dancers in deep aqua body suits doors shaking giant silver spheres. Somehow a noise like running water was coming from these spheres, blending well with the slower chants of the choir. They threw them back and forth to each other as they twirled and spun their way up the carpet.

Last came a wagon in the shape of a whale. The whole platform had to be the length of two chariots. Seaweed and reddish kelp twined around the frames, and shells encrusted into its sides made it look armored. Alowen only spared a glance at the old man and his wife sitting stiffly at the front of the wagon. Unlike other Alluran guests, they wore only their traditional bare minimum, the kind that allowed their people to cut through water easily. They bore their drab clothing dignifiedly, high above any embarrassment.

But Alowen was already looking past them. How could she have forgotten this was coming? Behind the royal couple sat someone whose face she had been seeing for days. It was the girl from her visions.

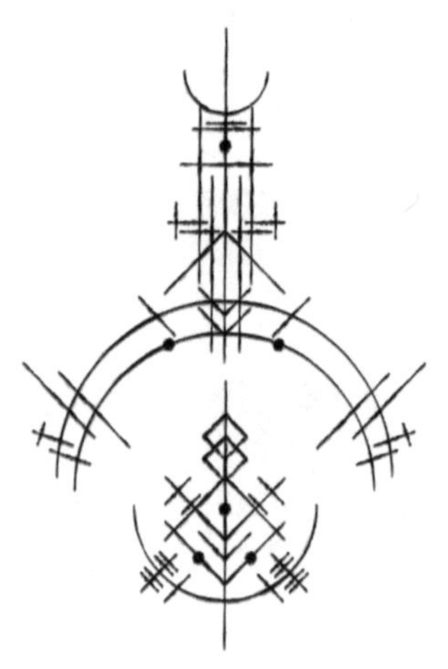

The princess' float seemed to pass in slow motion. Alowen couldn't look away. She looked nothing like she did in the visions—fragile, shivering, utterly miserable. Here she sat straight and regal on a deep blue cushion shaped like a starfish. A tiara of violet coral fronds wrapped around her brow. Under it, her face was blank, and not just from any magical powder or rogue. Somehow, she had hidden her fear beneath a completely different girl, draped with a cloak that looked like a massive manta ray. Four of her maidens twirled around her to the warbling choir in robes of purple-red kelp. The whole group slowly reached the dais where the royalty got off their float and gracefully ascended the stairs. Then there were cheers and gasps as cables reached from the ceiling, hooked onto the wagon, and hoisted it up so it looked like the whale swam higher. Whoever manipulated the cables steered the whale beyond the dais, and applause thundered through the hall.

The dancers and choir before the stage bowed. The rattle of their instruments still filled the hall. But Alowen only had eyes for the princess' distant form. So, she was definitely hallucinating the past few days? But it didn't make sense, everything she had seen was so sequential, and so real.

"Why are you frowning?"

She blinked and turned toward the voice.

"You look upset. What's wrong?" Soren pointed out.

She almost couldn't hear him over the noise, but he had an eyebrow raised. Uhh…

"My mother," she admitted. "I wish she were here." And it was true, not just an excuse. She tried to shake away the images of the princess, both from the visions and the float. Keep talking; keep talking. "She, ah, didn't want me to come at first, you know?"

Soren paused. "But…?"

You've always been so excited to get to the "finished result," but when it comes to becoming the best version of you, you will never be finished. I wish I could show you through my eyes how much you've grown, how quickly. You've got this, Alowen. You are going to do so well in Bachha.

"But I guess she realized she couldn't keep me from my dreams." Oh no, she was actually tearing up. Alowen tilted her head back to stop the tears from falling. "It was hard for her, but I am so glad…" Thankfully, she caught something out of the corner of her eye, and turned back to the procession before Soren could speak.

"Here comes the Arbor."

A thundering percussion rolled across the hall before the startling figure of a tree with swaying branches walked heavily into the room. It was at least twenty feet tall, and as it approached Alowen made out dozens of bodies clinging to each other. The silhouettes at the top were dressed entirely in shades of dark green to create the illusion of a canopy, and they gently swayed back and forth as the tree lumbered forward. With the loud boom of the percussion, a new crew of dancers ran up to the tree plucking fruit and nuts from the branches and dropping them into baskets in their fellows' arms. Their movements were fluid, their balance steady. The room burst into applause, but it wasn't over.

More dancers leapt into the room. The lead was dressed like a deer with a full head of antlers, several others behind him slunk and crept along the floor in fur pelts, resembling wolves, and finally the last few dancers looked like the famous hunters of the Arbor. The Earth people had been telepathic partners with various creatures in their hunts for generations. The "deer" led the "wolves" and people around the tree for a lap or two before finally being brought down.

The room generously cheered.

The mayor of the Arbor came in last wearing an evergreen cloak with a hood over a grey wool suit. He waved to each side of the room as he walked toward the stage, smiling as the people cheered and waved back.

"Same old Marrow?" Soren asked.

"Yes, same old Marrow."

She watched the Arbor's mayor make his way up to sit, with his councilmen. The old man wasn't much of a genius, and he didn't show his face much, but taxes were the lowest they had ever been with him in office. She would miss him once he retired.

Next, the hall gasped as long spindly figures spiraled and swung from the ceiling on white silk ribbons, flipping and twirling ten feet overhead. Each had winged costumes, symbolizing them as eagles. Below the aerial troupe stood two people in snowy, white cloaks gesturing with shepherd crooks as a ceremonial nod to their ancestors who tended goats before they tamed eagles and built their great mountain city. They looked like holy sages with cosmic wisdom like the legend said. If only the real ones could see how their descendant councilmen debated emptily over important topics while berry pickers died and mixed Element workers begged for more pay.

Her words to her mother floated back. *This whole business*

of being an adult is tougher than I thought! And the world was weirder, more complicated than she thought when she first left home. Supposedly good, wise adults didn't care if the more unfortunate suffered. Her eyes went to Frazyk walking behind the performers, waving, and smiling brightly at the cheering hall. He had refused his personal orb to travel with the people. He had advocated for the Element Liaison Federation, finding simplicity and happiness within singlehood. Somehow this man she respected so much had overcome the difficult stress of adulthood. At least that gave her some hope.

Finally, the Sky performers ended their act, Frazyk mounted the steps, and the candles dimmed rapidly once more. As the hall went nearly pitch black, horns blared. Invisible drums pounded away, and applause rocketed through the hall again.

A group of fire dancers burst into the room hall, their bodies coated with bright pink fire. More and more poured in until there were twenty in a circle, only a short arm's reach from the nearest tables. Two dancers met in the center and began circling each other to the drumbeat. Each tossed their hands up, pink fire forming all manners of patterns and shapes against the dark ceiling; a spinning wheel, an eagle soaring over the dais, a horse-drawn chariot. The audience clapped and wowed over each new conjuration. At some point, the center dancers whipped up a hoop that the others jumped and rolled through.

Finally, all twenty raised their arms and with a whoosh of air and flame, created a spiky conch shell that looked like the one surrounding their city. It held for a dazzling minute before they extinguished it, just as the candles around the hall lit back up. Mayor Merritt and his son strode past the dancers who fell in line behind them. Both were smiling and waving with enthusiasm. Alowen had to admit, they looked like handsome copies of each other in their matching crimson suits. Once the two seated themselves, a Bachhan man in a smart waistcoat walked up to the front of the stage.

"Ladies and gentlemen, citizens of the Four Elements, it is my greatest pleasure to welcome you to this year's Element Party! Once again, we are here to celebrate the existence and perseverance of the Four Elements even so many years after the Frozen Years…"

As the emcee droned away, Alowen noticed Soren looking at the stage. His eyes were pleasant, but his jaw was clenched. He seemed so distracted, he didn't notice her.

"…Once again, this Party couldn't have been possible without the generosity and prosperity of our Bachhan organizers and sponsors…"

She glanced around the table. Everyone listened intently to the opening speech. She leaned over and tapped Soren gently.

"Now it's your turn to look upset. What is it?"

"Sorry"—he picked up his glass and gestured around the grand auditorium—"just…all this talk about the Party's lavishness." He sipped the merlot like it was vinegar. "Meanwhile, if you knew how hard it was for my mother to even rent a house because her kid is mixed."

Alowen's face fell as she stared at him. All these posh settings had to be salting his wound.

"Even before she got sick, we barely had money for food. Since we didn't have any extended family in the Arbor, we had no help. Her parents both passed when she was young, and my dad's family stopped speaking to my mom when he died in an accident with a shark." He cleared his throat. "No one in town wanted to rent her a place to live. One landlord made her promise not to tell anyone I was mixed, and he was the only kind one. Then she got sick, so I started working nights in a bakery downtown just to get a little extra money for food. No one helps you when you are a mixed Element. Everyone wants to pretend we don't exist. The neighbors all knew how sick she was, and they wouldn't even look at us." He looked down at his hands crossed around his glass. "Then she passed away. I didn't know what to do at first. So, I decided to go work in Wolken. I cleaned the house out and sold it, and now here we are."

He looked at her briefly and then down again.

"Soren…" She choked. "I'm so sorry about your mom, and everything you went through."

Her words felt empty and pointless. What could you say to someone who had lived through that? She had no idea things were so tough for mixed Element people. She couldn't imagine having no help at all in that situation.

"Excuse me, you two." She jumped and spotted the Wolken banker frowning at them. "If you young people aren't going to listen to the speech, could you at least keep your whispers down?"

Next to him, Mrs. Rosseur shook her head. "They have obviously never been to one of these before. No sense of respect for this function."

Alowen bit her lip. No way was she going to snap back and make a scene, no matter how tempting.

Soren's eyes were murderous, but he forced a tight smile. "I apologize."

His face was back to being pleasant, their conversation over. Alowen sipped her drink and eyed him again. The merlot made her tongue momentarily numb.

For years she had been living cozily in the Arbor thinking she knew everything there was to know about the place, but there was so much she didn't know about the mixed Element people who lived in it. When this was all over, she had to find some way to help. Somehow.

"And with that," said the emcee, "please join me in raising a glass to the eternal celebration of the Four Elements and the harmony amongst our diverse peoples. The banquet may commence."

Around them, people rose to their feet. Alowen pushed back her chair and stood too, trying not to look at Soren. The Party had barely started and already she felt uncomfortable.

"To Life and Warmth everlasting!" The emcee toasted the room, and they called it back to him, raising their flutes. Everyone except Alowen and Soren clinked and drank. She saw a few of Sal's group scowling and not drinking either.

"To lifelong enjoyment of the seasons!" The room roared back.

Alowen slipped a look toward the dais. The Alluran king and queen seemed to be in some disagreement with the king constantly nudging a glass toward his daughter. The girl stood and looked down at the Alluran table with folded hands.

"To unity across elements!"

With each toast the guests sounded off louder and more enthusiastic. Waiters slipped in and out amongst the tables, refilling glasses.

"And last but not least"—the emcee lifted his toast high above his head—"to strength in diversity!" A large chorus of cheers and claps filled the auditorium, and the bell tinged again. "Please, please, take your seats. Let dinner be served!"

More waiters appeared, balancing platters of porcelain bowls on their shoulders piled high with their banquet.

"Excuse me, miss, coming through." One of them placed his platter between Alowen and Soren, and a buttery, mushroom aroma floated toward her.

"That smells excellent." Her stomach growled.

The oldest Arbor recipes made their mushroom soup with beef strips and croutons, but the Bachhans seemed to serve theirs with chunks of an odd textured meat. She sniffed at it curiously.

"That's baby octopus," Soren told her, taking spoonfuls. "I would eat it raw but"—he shrugged and bit one of the chunks—"caramelized isn't so bad."

"My favorite is the pork shoulder with the roasted beets and crackling skin," beamed Mr. Rosseur. He was already red in the face but still beckoned a waiter for a refill of his empty glass. "And wait till course fifteen when they bring out the seven layered cheesecake." He shivered in bliss. "That alone is more than enough reason to enjoy yourself."

Course seventeen? Alowen wanted to ask how on earth they were going to make it through course eight, but Mr. Rosseur had already returned to his soup. She frowned. No one ever talked about how airheaded and indulgent the upper class were. Maybe Soren's story just made it more apparent.

Back in the Arbor, even the wealthiest landowners didn't treat luxuries this nonchalantly. She had to admit, the mushroom soup was delicious—although the tentacles were a bit alarming in comparison to the stews she was used to. Alowen spooned up as much as she could because the waiters were already on their way with the next course. This one was a basket of fried quail with a dressing of limes and coconut milk. Then came a steamed cod almost three feet long stuffed with figs and walnuts. By the fourth course, fried rice with grilled beef served in pineapple bowls, Alowen could hardly breathe in her dress. It was all so exquisite but so much. How did these people do this?

She giggled politely at some joke a Bachhan winemaker said across from them. Frazyk had Mayors Merritt and Marrow laughing loudly beside him. Exactly how drunk was he right now?

Surprisingly, Leiland's seat was empty. When did he

leave? And where? Down the table all three members of the Alluran royal family were sitting stiffly, barely eating let alone talking. It wasn't surprising—most Allurans could stomach and even learn to like foreign foods, all but the element's most conservative. But still, none of them looked like they were enjoying themselves. The princess had her face turned down into her lap.

Maybe it was the rich food, how sad she looked, or how much people around her contrasted with Soren's life, but suddenly the hall felt suffocating. The doors were calling. Alowen slid her chair back and lurched to her feet.

"Miss?" Mr. Rosseur asked. "Where are you going?"

"I'd like to get some fresh air." She drained her glass.

Thank goodness she didn't have to interview anyone. She made her way over to the entrance, passing waiters and candles.

"You look exquisite, young lady," someone drawled at her. She ignored him and kept walking.

Out in the foyer there were people who had left the hall too. Some lit cigars and pipes, while others leaned against each other, laughing and caressing. They must be quite drunk. Hopefully they find some place private before they go too far.

She leaned against a pillar and exhaled. She felt drained by the scene, except for Soren. She learnt more about him tonight than she had her whole school life. She looked back at the banquet hall. All these elitists who could vacation somewhere nice for months or afford to live in Bachha and meanwhile people struggled to get by just for being in mixed Element relationships.

She chuckled, a little bitterly. She didn't have to worry about offending anyone here, their attention seemed to pass over those less powerful than them. All the stuffy, ladder climbing people were meaningless to her. The people who did matter were people like Soren. She wished she knew what to say to him.

"Encore! Encore! Let's hear more!" erupted from outside followed by a round of hooting and shouting.

The rest of Bachha must be having the time of their lives. She walked over to a set of double windows. Down the road there was a podium with a well-endowed woman in a corset dress bellowing out poetry to a raptly attentive crowd. She couldn't make out the individual words, only the sporadic shouts of appreciation. More stages and stalls had been set up across the street from the palace, and the road was jammed with folks. Here and there were clearings where dancers whirled and flipped. She even saw a few cartoonish costumes of fishes and birds wandering about. In the distance, she caught a flash of green, fiery sparkles shooting high.

How did Bachhans have the energy for these night long celebrations? Alowen started to head for the door before she caught herself. She couldn't leave like this, Frazyk wouldn't know where to find her later. Instead, she went for a flight of stairs wide enough to fit a piano. Even the third floor would be high enough to show her what's happening blocks away. Up two flights, moving around the occasional couple who left the hall to indulge themselves, she found a large window overlooking the streets. Alowen sat on the broad sill behind long curtains.

A row of papier mâché "pets" were set up at a starting line. A young man holding a bright red flag suddenly shouted "GO!". Away they raced down the center of the road while crowds on either side cheered. A pink elephant with a polka dotted trunk was in the lead followed by a rather menacing frog with large black wings, and finally what looked to be a beaver with a bright red tail. It was bumbling slowly in last place.

"And the winner is, Mrs. Dots!" The apparent owner of the elephant rushed to scoop her into his arms, twirling her around with delight.

Suddenly, soft footsteps sounded over the landing, and then a shrill, wavering voice interrupted her thought.

"Alright, three flights are enough. I'm too old for this." The man sounded just three feet away.

"Fine," someone else grumbled. "But keep your voice down, alright? And talk in code. Even up here we need to be careful."

This voice sounded familiar and Alowen frowned, concentrating. She shouldn't be eavesdropping, but it would be awkward to move now.

"Well, Leiland, it must be really important if you went through all this trouble of pulling me from retirement to talk someplace this secret. What's this about? You're not relapsing again?"

Leiland? Alowen's eyes widened, and her heart pounded.

"Gollo, stop it. I haven't relapsed since you rehabilitated me those twenty years ago," Leiland muttered impatiently. "This is about"—he seemed to wrestle with himself—"a young friend of mine. Her partner got her pregnant, and her parents…they shouldn't find out."

"And you need an aged, long forgotten doctor to deliver the child." The other man sounded amused. Leiland coughed. "I also need this doctor's large, comfortable house for my friend to stay after the Party. Only two months."

Silence. "Come on, stingy, you're rich. You can afford her room and board. And you're retired and living alone. I'm doing this for you, too."

The old man sighed. "Fine, but I can't believe you're making me wait here. I can't stand Bachha." Alowen could feel Leiland relax. "Thank you, old friend. Really, how can I ever—"

"Don't relapse at this party." Their footsteps started down the stairs. "So many drugs in this city, no wonder I hate it."

Alowen didn't know how long she stayed motionless. *The princess' face was pained as she swallowed chunks of fish.*

Lei's finishing his plans.

There was no one else. Tonight, her dreams were already proven true so…it had to be the princess… right? Still, even if it was true, there was something deeper than that. She could feel it. But what? Time to head back. She cast one more look at the window. A draining night, but this view just about made up for it.

Alowen got back to the banquet hall to find the music had changed. A woman's low voice from the next room crooned some ballad along with the slow tinkle of strings and flutes, but from a distance. People slowly wandered into the room. The Bachhan and the Alluran royalties had left, the long table empty.

"There you are!" Frazyk strode up to her, looking stern. "Where were you? I was about to send the staff on a search."

Alowen flushed. "I'm sorry, I lost track of time. I just went for some air and got distracted by the street view. I didn't mean to worry you."

He stepped back and breathed a sigh. "It's okay. You are safe, that's all that matters." He shook his head and signaled more wine from a waiter. "How's the Party for you so far?"

"It's…" She rubbed her brow, trying to think. The whole Leiland thing was so confusing and worrying. She'd have to process it later. "I love the food, but I got full so quickly, and I can't say I like the rich people," she blurted.

Frazyk burst into a hearty laugh. "The rich people huh? I do agree politics and money can be a bit…draining. Was there something, or someone, in particular that displeased you, Alowen?"

She frowned. "Well, that smug Mr. Rosseur was talking about buying land in the Arbor and building housing to make a profit. I doubt I need to explain why that's problematic." Her frown deepened. "But it ruins the habitats of our wildlife building like that, and it drives up the cost of homes. We haven't even finished discovering lands out there."

"Yes, yes." Frazyk wrinkled his brow. "Well, the food's free at least." He shrugged sheepishly. "Comes with the territory of all this…glitter. Can't pass that up, right?" His grin came back. "Hey, tell you what. Tomorrow, our presence isn't needed here as much as it was today. Let me take you around Bachha."

"Thanks, I'd like that." Alowen thought about the wild abandon people were having in the streets. Everyone seemed so much happier and lighter than anyone in here. "Thanks, Frazyk. I don't think I can handle being around the elite for a whole week."

"Well, you do have to interview more celebrities in the next few days." Frazyk smiled. "But yes, we'll make it tolerable for you, and you won't need to spend every waking moment with them. He offered his arm. "For now, perhaps you'll like to dance?"

"Dance?" Alowen took his arm doubtfully. She had only done it once at school, and she wasn't even sure she was in the mood now. "It's okay if you don't want to. But at least take a look. Maybe you can chat with some of Sal's entourage. Or maybe you'll find Wombat again, eh?" He gave her one of his winks, and she rolled her eyes.

"Okay, fine, I guess. If dancing comes with the chance of seeing Wombat again, I'm in."

Though truthfully, she had nearly forgotten about the three boys. Her little crush on Raydan was over, thanks to busyness and stress, but that was okay. He likely met way too many girls to actually be interested. Still, Wombat would be welcome company.

The singer sounded pleasant too, in a husky sort of mez-zo-tone. "In life's great showwww…I'm content…to be in the audience row, where I…watch the drama unfold…finding joy in stories untold…"

Alowen couldn't help but sway a bit to the music as she walked.

Frazyk chuckled. "There we go, you're relaxing."

"Hush." She nudged him with her elbow. "Let me enjoy the music."

"Yes ma'am." He bowed sarcastically.

They walked through the doors into a massive ballroom where at least thirty to forty couples were twirling gently in circles. Around them were even more people talking amongst themselves with a few joining on the dance floor. She noticed Sal dancing with a very well-dressed Bachhan woman who smiled intently at him. He spun her all the way around and gently dipped her as she laughed playfully. Here and there were a couple of his entourage with their own dance partners. Alowen watched them for a minute. They were teachers and singers and scientists. How did they feel about being around such privileged people when their own ruler and council kept them so regulated under restrictive laws?

She spotted Iris being spun by a gentleman, her lavender blue skirts sweeping in a graceful arc. Well, at least there was one person who seemed to embrace being amongst the wealthy.

"Mayor Frazyk!" An older lady came up to them, all glittery with earrings and pendants. Even one of her teeth winked silver. "When was the last we met? Not two Parties ago?"

Frazyk pretended to think. "Oh no, it can't be. Selena, where did the time go? Tell me you weren't on leave these two years."

He turned to Alowen. "I'll see you later, child?" Then he dropped his voice. "She's funded fifty construction projects across Wolken. I can't say no to more, can I?"

"Have fun." Alowen ran a hand through her hair as he walked over to Selena.

She really liked Frazyk, but after the Party, she would enjoy not being anywhere near politics. Too much brown-nosing. At least the night was winding down. She could get some coffee from a waiter and just rest somewhere before Frazyk took her home.

Unfortunately, her gorgeous dress wasn't doing her any favors. A gentleman older than Uncle Rogan walked up to her.

"Evening, miss, I can't help wondering if you would like a—"

Oh no. Alowen shook her head hastily. "I'm sorry, sir. I'm not feeling well."

She hurried away, hugging herself. Barely two minutes later, another man with a handlebar mustache reached his hand towards her.

"Hello, dear. Perhaps you and I can—"

"I have a dance with someone else. I'm sorry," she cut him off.

The problem was…who was this someone else? She scanned the crowd, her heart beating fast. She glimpsed a deep green tux several feet away. It was now or never. She shot the man an apologetic smile and brushed past him.

"Excuse me." As she got closer, Alowen gave a little bow to a woman in an orange dress who kissed Soren's cheek and patted his shoulder, saying, "Take care now."

He stuck his hands in his pockets sullenly. Alowen's curiosity climbed. But Soren noticed her first.

"Regular patronizing rich person who doesn't care about

anything outside their world."

Alowen paused. Soren understood more than anyone how frustrating it was, talking to brick walls like these.

"Well, it's late. It seems pointless to work now and I have strange men asking me to dance. Maybe it's safer if I dance with a friend?'

"Ladies and gentlemen, we'll be having our final number for this evening. My name is Chennesdel and it's been a pleasure to sing for your Opening Ball."

Soren shrugged. "Last one. Better than another dance with one of these elitists."

He held up a hand and after a pause, she took it. Oh! Uh… He placed his other hand on her waist. A jolt ran up her side from his touch and she pretended to cough as an excuse to turn away. Hopefully, he hadn't noticed her startled expression.

"I hope I'm not coming down with something."

"It's okay." Somehow his solemn face made her feel less awkward. "On three, we step toward my left."

"Right." She forced herself to look him in the eye. "On three."

"One, two, three." She followed as he swayed left. Then right, a little. Left again. She had to say, he moved gracefully.
I wear a mask to hide.
The world won't understand me, but you see past to what's inside.
For the first time I want you to see.

They moved slowly and deliberately together in a box-like motion. Alowen focused one foot at a time on following Soren's movements and soon they glided gracefully around the room. His hand felt strange, but warm, in hers. She wasn't sure where to look. Oh, this was stranger than she thought! It's not like they were ever as close as they were in that moment.

"I—I have a question." She cleared her throat. "Um,

what can you tell me about Leiland?"

He tilted his head, clearly surprised. "Someone's been telling you old gossip stories about the mayor's son?"

Curiosity washed over her embarrassment. They turned, again and again. "Well, no. I—He just seems a bit mysterious. Just…what do you know about him?"

"Look, this is what I've heard, so don't quote me. Supposedly, Leiland used to have a pretty bad problem with addiction, and he got himself in quite a bit of trouble. He's been sober quite a number of years now, but I think he's had some trouble bringing his reputation back to good standing. I know he had some issues with women. You know, too many girlfriends. A lot of cheating. At one point, he was caught placing illegal bets and could have gone to jail, but his family bailed him out very quickly. I think it wouldn't be as big of a deal if he weren't the mayor's son."

For a moment, she considered telling him what she had heard, and all her past visions. But where to even start?

"Well, I would never have guessed looking at him now. He's changed so much."

"I think he means well." Leiland shifted, and she braced herself just before he twirled her. "He just wasn't his best self when he struggled with addiction."

"I'm surprised." They just narrowly missed another couple. "You don't dislike him? I thought because of his past and privilege…"

"No, I don't dislike him at all. It's not his fault he was born into privilege, no more than it's our fault we weren't. It's also not his fault he's an addict. It's a disease, you know. I think it's really admirable he's managed to stay sober all these years. He's even gotten involved a bit in helping with the Alluran liberals. He's introduced us to some people willing to support our movement."

He's truly seen a lot, more than she knew. And still he's

trying to help.

"You are a good man too, Soren," she said softly. "I really believe in what you and Sal are doing."

"Thank you, Alowen." Soren straightened his lapel. He looked completely solemn, but he spared her another smile.

"Good night now."

Alowen turned away, her cheeks burning. Her arms suddenly felt cold without his touch. She had barely noticed they were dancing; she'd been paying so much attention to their conversation. People moved by her, and she blinked. Right, she had to find Frazyk. Still, her mind stayed on the sway and swing of the last few minutes. Though it felt shorter. Too short. Maybe because it was the first slow dance she had in years or because Soren made it feel so easy.

She found Frazyk wishing people good night. Everyone looked like such good friends, laughing and joking as they parted ways.

"Take care, old friend." He clapped a man on the shoulder, turning to her. "Ready?"

"Yes, definitely."

Her whole day had been socializing almost nonstop. It was time to relax on her own. He took off his hat and brushed it off, a comical dent left in his tall hair.

"Well, you sound tired. Thankfully, a lot of people have left even before this and the carriage moves fast. We'll be back in twenty minutes." He chuckled at her expression. "It'll feel shorter than that, hopefully. Come." He waved at a waiter. "Two chamomiles, please." Without missing a beat, he started for the banquet hall, and she followed. "Well, did you get to dance with anyone? Or put anyone in their place?"

Alowen smiled tiredly. "Two guys, thirty times my age, tried to invite me and I told them no. Then I saw Soren and decided to pick him. At least, no one else would ask me while I was dancing with him." She caught a rising smirk on Frazyk's face. "Hey no, Frazyk, come on. It wasn't like that. It's only a dance."

"Only a dance, ha." Frazyk accepted a chamomile from the waiter, who then handed Alowen another. "There's another pair I know who once said those words." He sipped his tea. "And look where we are now."

Alowen stared at him. He managed half a sullen smile back at her before he looked down at the cup in his hand. "You asked me once if I ever wanted to have a partner. Years ago, when I was still assistant to the Wolken Mayor's office, Adenike and I tried."

Alowen froze. This was it. This was the truth behind the mystery.

"It started with a waltz during another Party. We thought it was only a dance, but it gave us a special connection forever. From that, I knew she was someone I wanted to know better. Over time we learned it just isn't practical in the real world."

Alowen blinked, "Wh—what do you mean it isn't practical? What happened?"

Frazyk looked at her distantly. "We met again later through work. She was writing a piece about the council in Wolken. We picked up where we left off from the dance, and it was beautiful. But she was a mixed race, and we were in the public eye, so it was tough. We tried to keep it a secret for several years, but rumors spread. Even worse, Wolken was discriminating more harshly on mixed Element people. Even the mayor's family had a shocking scandal."

SCANDAL - MAYOR DROW HUMILIATED; DAUGHTER FOUND ROMANTICALLY ENTANGLED WITH MIXED-ELEMENT PAINTER, TENNO MORICE

Adenike's note flashed back to her. *It's getting serious. Tenno told me he's been getting hate mail everywhere. He's leaving the city today, and I hear the mayor has sent his daughter to boarding school somewhere just outside Allurus. I am scared, Frazyk.*

"Eventually, she was passed over for a promotion because of those rumors, and I just couldn't have that. She is such an incredible talent. I couldn't allow my selfishness to ruin her career. So, we remained friends."

He drained his tea. It made sense now. Both of their behaviors when thinking about the other, the silences, the news clipping, and the note.

"I'm sorry you both had to go through that, Frazyk. I can see why you love her. I mean, loved her." She flushed.

Choosing between career and love must be so tough, but she didn't blame them for sticking with their careers. How unfortunate to live in a time that frowned on mixed Element relationships.

Frazyk smiled gently. "Be careful of certain relationships. That boy is the right-hand man of one of Allurus' most unpopular ambassadors. I told you once, when you are both up and rising you figure out quickly love doesn't mix well with that."

She wasn't sure what to say. But she was definitely not in any place to think about a relationship. Soren was just a friend, after all.

Frazyk held his cup up for a waiter. "Let's get you back to the hotel, shall we?"

***

Dear Mom,

I miss you so much! How are things there? How is Uncle Rogan? The last few days have been so busy! I was worried I wouldn't find time to write, honestly, but I'm finally alone for a few minutes. I can't wait to take a trip with you here, to Bachha. It's so beautiful and so different from the Arbor. Frazyk has been giving me a bit of a tour when we aren't at events for the Element Party. The other day we visited the Alluran underwater observatory. They have an octopus nursery! I even got to hold one! He also took me to a famous bakery here called Poof. You order your muffin, they bring it to your table uncooked, and then they cook it instantaneously with their fire! I ordered cranberry orange because I miss your cooking. (They weren't as good as yours I promise.) You wouldn't believe how late everyone stays up here. It's like daytime around the clock with all of the performers, food, and drinking. The other night I heard a commotion, and I peeked out into the street and saw some people racing those papier mâché pets after midnight! There was a huge crowd, and everyone was wearing such incredible outfits, so many colors. You would enjoy this, but the noise does get to be a bit much, and the crowds. Luckily, it's quiet in the hotel so I can rest.

I think I am finally getting the hang of interviewing celebrities. You know Zolta? The famous Wolken play actress? She practically told me her whole life story. Did you know both of her parents passed away in cloud berry picking accidents? Tragic. I love learning so much about people, but at the end of each day I can't wait to get back to the hotel where no one can talk to me! As much fun as this is (and it has been such fun), I am just as excited to come home and see you. I will fill you in on the rest of the details in a couple days when I get there.

Love you so much! Tell Uncle Rogan I said hello,

Alowen

Alowen sat back with a relieved sigh and started shuffling her articles. Thirty articles done, one for each celebrity guest in over just a few days. Wow, that felt good. She couldn't wait to show Adenike. She placed her work down and looked at the chandelier. It was wild to imagine that tomorrow she would be back home. But first, there was the Closing Night ceremony. She took a look at the clock and got up. Two hours should be enough to get ready. After that, it's one last night of eating fancy food and tolerating the rich, she could do that.

***

Alowen took a fifth sip of her fermented pear juice, wishing she was a bit tipsy at least. She couldn't listen to one word of stocks and equity and liquefying assets any longer.

She took a glance at the stage where Frazyk and Merritt sat. Leiland had disappeared a long while ago, and the Alluran royals had departed some twenty minutes ago. The poor princess looked so uncomfortable during the Closing Night Procession in a hooded cloak that looked like a fuzzy, red anemone, but hopefully she got to take it off now.

Mr. Nuest on her right was asking her about how she would feel to own the deeds to a lovely villa around the west coast of the old Bachhan island.

She offered him an apologetic smile. "Please, excuse me. I'll be right back."

How did she land at a table of bankers and investors for Closing Night? Soren gave her a sympathizing smile and shrug, and she shrugged back. Ten minutes by herself would do. She wandered out with her glass in hand and made her way up to the fifth floor, staring out at the buoyant sight below. The past few nights had been unbelievable. One day she would come back here.

Something moved in the corner, behind a heap of props and various painted stage sets. She nearly jumped. Was there some creature here?

"Hello? Who's there?" Alowen called into the shadowy corner, her stomach churning. A tattered piece of tan cloth draped across the floor was swiftly yanked back behind the pile of what looked like stage props. She walked closer. "Hello?"

"I need help," came a soft, feminine voice as a green face peeked from behind the junk.

Alowen felt a wave of confusion as she recognized the princess, barely visible beneath the rags wrapped over her head and around her body. Was this a disguise?

"Princess Ilya? Is that you? What's going on?"

A tear fell from the princess' eye, and she wiped it with a trembling hand.

"Alowen?" Alowen jumped a foot in the air as a male voice appeared behind her. She turned swiftly, her body in a fighting stance, until she saw Leiland.

"Leiland! What is happening?"

His expression wore fear and urgency.

"There's no time, I'm sorry. I'll see you around." He moved past her and tenderly helped the princess to her feet.

"Wait, no, where are you taking her?" Alowen's heart started to thump. "What is happening? Why is the princess here? Are you okay, Princess?" She turned to the girl who shook in the shadows.

"How do you know her?" Leiland asked, his tone suspicious and stiff.

Alowen realized she was unprepared to explain her visions. "Everyone knows who the princess is. What do you mean?"

His face relaxed a little, but he shook his head. "Really sorry we don't have time, Alowen. The princess is in danger, and we have to go right this second. That's all I can tell you. Unless you come with us."

She stopped. Go with them…? Where? No. No, that

was ridiculous. Leave everything? Even after what Soren said about Leiland, and how good a person he seemed…

Leiland seemed to be struggling too. "Look," he finally said. "We need to get her out of Bachha or she will be caught. And possibly harmed. That's the short version. Can we trust you to help us?" He held out his hand, his eyes pleading.

She hesitated, but how could she say no? They seemed so afraid. "What can I do?"

Leiland looked worriedly around the room. "Just stay with her here for a minute. As soon as the coast is clear, I will come and grab you both. There is a tunnel we can use to get to the bottom floor of Bachha, and then I have a way to get us out. We have to move fast." He paused. "Well, we could hide in the secret passageway where we came from until the search teams have moved out of the Palace. That would be safer…"

Then he shook his head and glanced at the princess. "No, we need to move fast. Stay here."

"Where will we go?" Alowen whispered harshly, but he hurried down the stairs, a few steps at a time.

All of Alowen's hair stood on end as a booming voice erupted up. "Stop! Don't move! Under Code 888 you are under arrest in suspicion of attempted kidnap of Bachhan Royalty. Do not resist or we will be forced to harm you."

Alowen froze and her blood ran cold as her mind raced. She ran to the corner where the princess was hiding and shoved both of them behind the stack of props. She put her finger silently to her lips as she stared into the princess' terrified eyes and quieted her breathing with every hunting technique she knew.

One noise from either of them would get them both caught. They were certainly trapped, but there was a slim chance they wouldn't be found. From downstairs came shouts and a scuffle as Leiland was surely being dragged away.

"You will regret this!" came his voice.

"I doubt that, sir!" replied the same man. "You have no idea just how much trouble you are in."

"Do you know who my father is?"

"Leil?" whispered the princess behind her as Leiland's voice thundered up the stairs. "Lei?" Her voice got louder. "Leiland??"

"Shush!!" Alowen grabbed her shawl desperately. "Please! Keep quiet!" The girl closed her mouth but teared up and trembled. Alowen immediately felt guilty, but she had no choice. She closed her eyes and listened for pounding steps. Nothing. There were still angry voices downstairs, but they were moving away.

She thought quickly and waved the princess toward the window. "Here! Over here." She slipped the long, thick curtains apart and hurriedly ushered her onto the sill. "Come on, stay here for a bit. Please wait quietly. I'm serious, don't move till I come back."

And with that, she started down the steps quietly. There were still a few couples in the foyer, but they were all staring at the banquet hall. No one gave her a second look as she slipped by them and snuck a peek through the doors. A sharp gasp slipped out.

There must be two dozen Allurus men in the hall, and about four people in their iron grasp. They were raising an uproar.

"What's the meaning of this?" a man shouted, struggling.

He looked like Professor Buerroca, a scholar of marine exploration.

"You have no right!" another person yelled as the Allurans hauled him away. "You have no right!"

"I'll be talking to your king about this!" Mayor Merritt threatened from the dais.

His fire burned deep pink, and a couple of people were keeping him back from the men. One of the Allurans turned to him. Alowen couldn't see his face, but there was definitely a smugness in his voice. It was the one who had arrested Leiland.

"Actually, our king commanded it." The hall came to a complete stop.

"Excuse me?" someone asked.

Maybe it was Merritt. Or even Frazyk.

The Alluran sneered. "He said to ask your son where his daughter is. Come!" His men began dragging away their captives.

"Stop! Stop!" a few of Sal's people cried, grabbing at some soldiers' arms.

To Alowen's shock, Sal was also being dragged off. The soldiers gave them glares.

"Even you…progressives…know better than to interfere with royal arrests."

"But he hasn't done anything. He's an ambassador. He's a good—"

"Save it! This man is wanted to answer to the throne for the missing princess."

The commotion carried on, and Alowen spun away, horrified. Everything was happening so fast, so wildly. What could she do? What *must* she do? She had to go on with her promise to Leiland. It was too frightening to think about what she had seen.

She started to make her away across the foyer when a hand grabbed her arm tightly. She was so startled she didn't even scream. Alowen turned to see Soren right behind her, his face tight with anger.

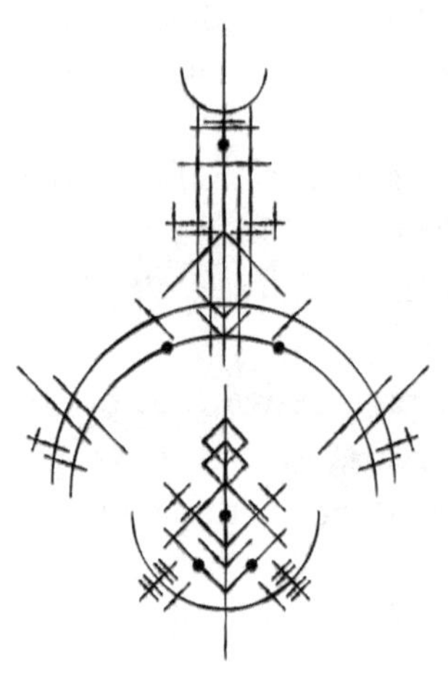

"Alowen, where have you been? I've been looking for you everywhere. You can't stay out here anymore. There's royal Allurus business going on. Frazyk's even sent some people out looking for you."

Soren's harsh tone stung a bit, but she couldn't blame him. She looked down at her shoes as her thoughts raced, struggling for an explanation. She wasn't sure if telling him everything was a good idea.

His tone changed as he took in her face. She shifted her weight and started to speak, but he cut her off.

"You need to get back to our table right now before they say you are involved in whatever this is." He started aggressively shuffling her off toward the banquet hall, but she pushed back against him with both arms and stood firm.

"Soren, please listen to me. I have something I need to tell you, and I need your help, but please listen before you say anything."

Just then came a scuffle and shouting in the banquet hall.

"I don't have time."

He shoved her gently toward a darkened corner and looked past the doors. When he pulled his body back, his face was beaded with sweat. Alowen peeked in too and covered her mouth in horror. Guards were dragging a barely conscious Sal across the floor. His coat was torn at the arm and his lip was bloody. Soren turned back with a sick look on his paled face, his fists clenched.

"I've got to help him," he murmured as he started toward the scene.

In a panic, Alowen bolted toward him and put her body in his way. "No. If you go in there right now they are going to take you too. You can't fight all of those guards, Soren."

He strained to slide past her, still staring at Sal. "No, Soren, listen to me." She began gently pulling him back into the corner. "Please, listen. This situation is dangerous for all of us. There is a lot going on, and I will tell you more, I promise. Come upstairs with me so we can come up with a plan? We need to get away from these guards before they catch us next." He glanced at her, then back toward the room where Sal was being carried away, and then at her again. "Please." Alowen's eyes pleaded.

Finally, Soren nodded, looking defeated. "Okay…"

The stomp of boots faded; they must be taking him in for questioning.

"Thank you for trusting me. Let's go."

Alowen led them upstairs toward the princess, her mind racing. How would she explain this? After several flights of stairs, they came onto the fifth landing and Alowen led Soren over to the windowsill and slipped the curtains apart. The princess jerked back with a small shriek and covered her mouth.

The grimness on Soren's face turned to horror as he spotted the princess. There was total silence for a minute as Alowen stumbled over her words.

"I tried to tell you; she's in trouble. I think it has something to do with Leiland. I think she might be…pregnant." They both looked at each other and then to the stunned, silent princess. "Please, we have to get her out of here, or

I'm scared they will hurt her, maybe even worse." Alowen's eyes begged.

Soren threw both arms up. "Alowen, the Princess of Allurus? What have you gotten us into?"

"Us? Are you saying you will help?" She held her breath.

His face was stark as he stared at a wall, pacing back and forth. What if he decided to turn them in instead? She couldn't blame him for not wanting to be wrapped up in a scandal. She gripped the wall to steady herself, her stomach churning with tension. The princess was trembling as she watched.

Finally, Soren sighed. "I suppose I don't have a choice, do I?"

She felt a wave of relief.

"We have to go right now. They are looking for her, for us."

Before thinking, Alowen grabbed him in both arms and hugged him, pressing her face in his chest.

"Thank you," she whispered.

He awkwardly accepted the hug. "Alowen, we have to get out of here." He peeled her away and motioned to the princess. "Please, we have to stay very close together now. I"—he looked around the fifth floor desperately—"I…wait, let me think."

"Excuse me…" came a weak voice behind them, startling Alowen. "Where is—where is Lei? I need to tell him I am okay."

This was the first time she'd heard the princess speak. She couldn't tell her what had happened, what if the stress made her sick? "We will tell him soon, okay? Right now, we just need to get you somewhere safe."

She felt guilty for lying. There was no way they could get Leiland any kind of message if he was locked in a jail somewhere, or worse. The princess nodded feebly.

"Alright." Soren was rooting around a heap of costumes in a dusty corner. "If we—Ah, here. Put this on." He handed Alowen a long white scarf and a hat from the heap before grabbing a bowler hat and a pair of glasses with a slightly bent rim. "No, like this." He covered the bottom of Alowen's face with the scarf. "The princess looks alright wrapped up like she is. Okay, let's go." He put his finger to his lips as he looked at them both and headed for the stairs.

Alowen's legs slightly shook with adrenaline as she guided the princess in front of her. They walked silently in single file, barely allowing themselves to breathe. Laughter rang ahead of them. What if someone from the party recognized her? How many people had Frazyk told to look for her? Ahead of her, Soren's body stiffened. He turned to them and widened his eyes in warning before moving again. She let out a sigh as she saw it was a few teenagers playing with papier mâché pets.

They were almost to the foyer now, and Soren was slinking like a house cat, keeping his body so close to the wall Alowen could hear his shirt scraping against the stone. Just around the corner she heard the deep murmur of male voices. Soren took a glance and turned back to them.

"There are guards there," he whispered. "There is no other way through. Maybe these disguises will be enough, maybe not. We have no other choice."

A bead of sweat trickled down beneath Alowen's scarf as she nodded. She glanced at the princess whose eyes seemed almost vacant. She couldn't imagine everything she'd been through and now having to run.

"Okay, let's go. Try not to talk." Soren straightened and walked confidently toward the doorway where three guards stood.

As they approached, one put up a hand. "Stop right there, son." The guards eyed the three of them a long time before two of them looked away. "Where are you heading to?"

"Lady Furlow sent us out for delicacies." Alowen was grateful for Soren's confident response. She didn't think she could manage to sound so calm. The guard grunted and stepped aside. Fresh air rolled in.

"Alright then, go ahead."

She noticed another one stared suspiciously at the princess but thankfully shrugged. Finally, they arrived at a line of carriages with their doors ajar.

"Quick, get in."

Soren lifted the princess inside first, and then Alowen shut the door gently behind him. He entered the coordinates of the Terminal into the cloud glass panel and took a deep breath. The roads started to sweep by with a rumble. Alowen stared at the glass numbly, barely thinking. What was she leaving behind?

***

The Terminal was having several blasts when they reached. Singing and stumbling crowds of party goers still lined the streets outside it, oblivious to their plight.

"Where are you off to in such a hurry, miss?" shouted an obviously intoxicated gentleman as he tugged at the frayed edge of Alowen's white scarf. "It can't be THAT important."

She tugged her scarf back from his clutch as he laughed after them. Her shoes stuck to the streets and made a noise like tape peeling each time she lifted her feet. The smell of spilt wine and food turned her stomach, adding to her anxiety. But Soren marched on next to her, his arm on the princess' shoulders. They went up the Terminal steps to where the gates stood.

"We are going to need a bubble up to the surface," Soren told a sentry. "This woman has suffered a serious case of claustrophobia. She needs some fresh air quickly."

He tightened his arm around the princess who kept her head down and her arms around her belly.

"Alright sir, not to worry." The sentry signaled to someone else a distance away. "We can get her medical attention right away." Alowen felt sweat down her neck and back. Oh no! No, no, no…They can't have that. Their heads would all roll in the next hour. All it would take was a proper officer from the Palace to come down.

"Sir, no. No." She waved her hand in the man's face, and he looked startled. "I'm sorry, but this girl really cannot take it in this shell any longer. The medical officer at the hotel already deemed her fit to head for the surface and feel the natural water and air. If we don't make sure she gets out…" She pointed at the princess, who really did look ready to faint any moment.

The sentry looked around uncomfortably, his hand still half-raised. "Well, hm…I suppose there was no time to issue a proper leave permit. Don't make me regret this." He unlocked his gate and stood aside as the bubble hatch opened. "The tides are heavy at night, but I'm programming this bubble to head for the shore and stay there thirty minutes. Make sure this girl recovers."

Alowen put her arm around the princess' waist. The girl was thankfully quite a bit shorter than her. She made sure her head was resting on her left shoulder.

"Come on, come on," she whispered, more to herself.

Any time now, Alluran and Bachhan officers could be speeding down the highway. Together she and Soren eased the princess down on a seat and hurriedly made her comfortable as the hatch closed. The bubble slid away through dark waters.

"Sit and watch her," Soren commanded.

He stood at the control console even though the bubble was clearly moving upward through the water without him. He kept staring down at Bachha as it shrank away below them, his fists clenched at his side. Alowen glanced down at Soren's clenched fist and choked back a tear. How could she drag him into all of this? What would happen now? After everything he had been through, losing his mother, now Sal in danger, his crew left without a leader. She wanted to apologize.

She didn't have the words. Instead, she turned back to the princess who sat with her knees drawn to her chest. Anxiously, Alowen reached out and fiddled with her scarf.

How far away was the surface? Could the sentries reverse the bubble if they found out the Alluran princess was in it? She tried her best to keep her own breath steady, but all she could hear was her own heartbeat. She closed her eyes and heard the swoosh noise. When she was little, she used to think her heartbeat sounded like a bird's wingbeat, but now the sound only agitated her further.

Come on, she urged the bubble silently. But it didn't speed up, and her heartbeat didn't slow. Her thoughts strayed back to Frazyk, miles away, with no idea of where she was. He must be terrified. He probably thought something terrible had happened to her, and he was responsible for keeping her safe. Not to mention the Element Party she had abandoned. This probably meant her career was over before it started. When word got back to The Arbor that she was missing, her mom and Rogan would be beside themselves with worry. She had to get a letter to them somehow so they would know she was safe. She wasn't sure it was possible, but she would find a way.

All three of them stayed that way for what felt like hours. Soren stood tensely, the princess stared blankly, and Alowen fiddled nervously. When the bubble finally rose out of the sea, the sight of the moon took Alowen by surprise. The pressure in her chest loosened slightly. The bubble pushed through the waves over to the shore, bobbing about from the force of the tides.

Tapping and clacking behind her made her turn around to see Soren working the console. "What are you doing?"

"Making sure the engines have maximum power." He grunted, twisting dials.

She couldn't tell if the bubble moved faster but maybe it helped him to be doing something. She could understand that. After an agonizing several minutes, the bubble finally bumped up against the shore, and the hatch slid open. The unfamiliar volcano loomed over them. In the dark it looked like the body of a sleeping dragon.

"Come on." Soren hurried over.

Together they ushered the princess from her seat, and outside onto dark, cold land. Alowen shivered the second she stepped out, and thoughts of warm, comfortable Bach-ha floated back in. If only she had grabbed a coat or something before she just ran away. She pulled the white scarf tighter around her neck. What was she thinking? For a moment, she looked back at the bubble. At least it was warm inside, but then she shook her head. Absolutely not. She had gone too far now; she couldn't turn back if she wanted. But where next? The bubble would head back down in thirty minutes, and once they saw it was empty…

In fact, the reports had probably already reached the terminal—it was their luck that the bubble didn't get recalled on its way up. She looked around urgently. They had to hide now. Soren seemed to have the same idea. He was guiding them further from the shore, deeper into the jungle. It was so dark though. She squinted ahead but aside from the figures next to her, she couldn't see anything.

"Soren. Soren!" She reached over the princess and tapped his shoulder. "Where are we going? I can't see!"

"Don't worry." Soren kept walking forward. "Just follow me, my eyes can see fine. Let's go ten feet in, there should be a tall tree we can rest under." That made sense. Allurans needed to see underwater. He pushed aside branches and brambles. "I know you are both probably tired, but…" He didn't need to finish.

Alowen tried her best to keep her head down as she walked so the branches wouldn't smack her in the face. Her legs ached since Soren had pointed out her tiredness. It must be the adrenaline and panic that kept her going. Roots and loose twigs cracked under her feet.

Sometime later, Soren came to a stop. "We should be deep enough." And indeed, they looked to be only a few feet from the volcano's side, with dense jungle blocking them from the shore. He sized up a palm tree. "This should be sturdy and wide enough." He patted the ground between two of its roots. "My princess, please sit. I am very sorry there isn't more we can provide."

The princess almost looked in pain, struggling to keep her eyes open. Her face held no relief, but the tension left her as she collapsed against the sand and drifted away. Alowen stared into the night sky, still stunned from the events of the day. The glistening beauty of the stars in the sky seemed to betray the moment. Their light was so steady, and her life was in shambles.

"Soren, I need to say something."

He momentarily looked up from a pile of twigs he was gathering to try for a fire.

"If I would have known what was going to happen, I would have—I would have lied to you. I would have…convinced you to leave."

He walked over and sat down next to Alowen, putting

his hand gently on her shoulder. "It's over now. We are here. Sal"—he shifted his weight—"Sal's been a good friend and mentor. Seeing him like that…" He cracked the twigs in his fist. "But after I saw you and knew something was wrong, I couldn't just leave you there alone. Anyways, you're not that good of a liar, are you?"

They chuckled, but there was no true laugh in it. Things just felt too heavy tonight. Still, for a second, she could breathe.

"I guess you're right. I'm not."

He got back up and struck a spark with his firestarter. "We can't have this fire too big so enjoy it while it lasts. They could be sending search parties anytime now."

It was good pragmatic strategy, but Alowen still wished she had brought hers. "So glad you kept that." Her smile was wistful.

He smiled back with sadness in his eyes. "We've come a long way since the Arbor, haven't we?"

Alowen nodded wordlessly, wondering if they would see it again. The small fire brought comfort and warmth. She could feel the heaviness of sleep dragging her away.

***

Alowen didn't know how long she slept, or rather how little. But when someone shook her lightly, she woke instantly. Beside her, the princess stirred as well. When she opened her eyes, she seemed even smaller than ever, huddled miserably inside her shawl.

The only light around was greyish white. "It's just before dawn," Soren whispered from a crouched position beside her. "Thankfully, it looks pretty cloudy today." His voice seemed to have turned hoarse. "I couldn't sleep so I kept watch all night. We must have gone in far enough at least because no one came by…yet."

She knew what that meant. Sooner or later, Alluran soldiers would be searching the island, maybe even today.

She couldn't put the question off anymore. "What are we going to do, Soren?"

Soren stood. "I also scouted around and found something. Follow me." The princess looked terrified, but he held up his hand. "It's okay, Princess Ilya. I checked three times. No one's coming anytime soon, and what I have to show you isn't far. Now come on. Stay close to the volcano."

Alowen shook her head. This better be some sort of magic portal back home. But she was too tired for joking, so she just got up, helping the princess to her feet.

***

After a while of brushing through the bushes and swatting away insects, Soren finally came to a stop. A modest farmhouse sat in a fenced clearing. It must belong to one of the older Bachhan families who wanted to stay on the island as caretakers. Small plots of earth, each the size of a mattress, lay spread across the bare land, looking like they had been raked. On the other side of the fence was another much grassier clearing, a small shed, and—

"An ash-goose." Alowen stopped. It clicked then. "Soren, this is insane. We don't know where we're going. We are tired and we don't—"

"I know, Alowen. I know," Soren rubbed one of his eyes. "And I have never flown on any bird, or even saddled one, but here we are. We got to try at least, before the farmer wakes up."

She tried to think, but it was useless. They had no other choice. "Alright. Is there a saddle anywhere? I've saddled Frazyk's eagle before."

It wouldn't be the same, but she kept that to herself.

"Yes, there's one in the shed. I checked." Soren smiled, probably from relief.

"Get it then. And Princess?" Alowen turned to clasp the girl's hands. "It's going to be alright. Y—you know?" What was it Adenike told her so long ago? "Take three deep breaths. Make sure your stomach is fully extended and let your breath out slowly, as slow as you can. Pull your shoulders down away from your ears." The princess looked doubtful, but she followed the instructions bit by bit. "Good, just like that." Alowen squeezed her hands lightly.

Alowen turned back to the ash goose which had wandered closer to the fence watching them curiously. Soren was coming over with the saddle.

"Alright, give it here." Alowen waited for him to reach her and then walked toward the goose with the saddle. It's beautiful, black neck was six feet long. Her neck and hands started to sweat. This was nothing like Tyrq, how could she even think this was possible?

You'll find yourself much more natural than you think,
I promise.

Alowen couldn't thank Adenike enough then. She had to try. It didn't work with Tyrq, but she had to. She took one last deep breath and took her last step. Now the fence only kept the goose and her about three feet apart.

"Hi there." She looked straight at the goose. "You are quite lovely, aren't you?" Nothing happened. The goose turned its head to look at her sideways, then honked. She almost jumped at the sound. "Shhh, it's okay. I'm safe, I promise." She tried to keep her voice steady as she inched closer, placing her palm flat against the divot where its wing met its side and gently scratched. The goose paused then kicked its foot a bit. "Ah, that's what I thought. That spot gets itchy, doesn't it?" All her time raising chickens turned out to be good for something after all.

"That's it, there we go…" she murmured, keeping her gaze on the goose's eye. "See? I'm your friend." Suddenly an idea came to her, and she began lifting the saddle like some offering. "It's okay. I won't hurt you."

The goose turned to look back down at her. Its bill could break her ribs with no problem. Alowen tensed, holding her breath. She had practiced this a bit with Uncle Rogan's hunting wolf, but she'd never quite gotten the hang of it. She closed her eyes and pictured herself, Soren, and the princess sitting comfortably in the saddle on the goose's back. She tried to create as much detail as she could with the wind rushing past them. She tried to add in warm, safe, feelings to convey trust to the goose. She placed the back of her palm gently to the crook of its neck and she felt an instant expansion of her own mind. It worked!

She blinked. She was back in the clearing, holding up a large saddle. The sky above was a dull grey. There was grass under her feet. On the other side of the fence, the goose sat, its back open to her, accepting her request.

***

"I had never seen anything like that before," said the princess as Alowen pushed the buckles into place and pulled tight on the straps.

The goose's back was a bit broader than Tyrq's and the saddle was bigger than Frazyk's, but at least they worked just about the same. How glad she was she practiced saddling Tyrq in Wolken.

Alowen couldn't help but smile. "I have never experienced anything like that before."

The princess looked down. "I always heard it was unnatural for people and animals to connect like that. But it didn't feel like that at all. It looked so peaceful and gentle and comforting."

Alowen could only nod at her. There was so much she wanted to say, but right now she didn't know where to start. She just went back to tightening the straps.

"Alowen, we should hurry." Soren's voice came behind her. "The dawn is coming." He was checking the windows of the farmhouse, making sure the farmer was still asleep.

"Let's go." Alowen looked at the goose, thinking quickly. "I'll get in front. Princess Ilya, you are behind me and hold tight to my waist. Soren, you are the back. Make sure you are both secure. Oh, and"—she had almost forgotten—"if you bend a little and let the wind flow over your back, you'll keep yourself a bit more secure."

The words caught in her throat as she remembered her first flight with Frazyk and Tyrq. It was hard to believe that was a mere two weeks ago. How excited she had been. How sheltered. What would Frazyk think of her now?

"And where are we going?"

She had forgotten all that. Where could they go? Home, to the Arbor? Not with her mom and Uncle Rogan there. She didn't want to lead Alluran soldiers to her house. To the unexplored wild lands? No. How safe was it there for three people with no food or extra clothes, and one of them pregnant.

Then it hit her.

The sky had turned orange and purple by the time a massive round platform was seen sticking out from the side of a thick, marbled wall in the mountains. Alowen held her breath as they circled it. Right now, it was too high up to see if there were any eagles on the meadow. They had been flying as high as they could all day, just in case they came across any orbs or eagles. But now, if they got caught here at the edge of Wolken, well, she was out of moves. She gently squeezed the sides of the goose with her knees, and it sounded a loud honk before slowly settling down lower and lower.

When they landed, everyone's legs were so cramped it took all of them several minutes to properly get off the goose. They each crouched on the grass, groaning and rubbing their shins. Alowen was the first to straighten up, even though she felt like an old woman.

"Princess Ilya?" Alowen walked over to the princess and rubbed her back. "I'm so sorry. We are done flying, so we'll be able to rest now."

Hopefully, Mr. Loggerman would give them refuge. If he said no, or worse, turned them in, then—then this was it. She waited for the princess to recover before carefully helping her stand and lean on her. Soren had managed to get his legs to work too by then.

"Come on."

Alowen led the way toward a ranch at the other end of the platform. The evening air was cool, the light fading faster. The cicadas had begun their serenade. Loggerman's ranch had the "closed" sign up, but Alowen banged on the door again and again. Finally, it opened, and the man stepped out, red in the face. His mustache was thick and intimidating, and he looked as hefty as an Arbor lumberjack.

"Can you read? Does it look like I'm open? Let me ask you again. Can. You. Rea—" He stopped in the middle of his rant and stared at the three of them. "Oh, my word." He looked like he had just been hit by lightning. "You better come in. Quickly."

Mr. Loggerman latched and bolted the door behind them before leading them through his front hall into his restaurant lit comfortably by his hearth. "The three of you made quite a mess of today." He switched on his giant pixilator, their faces appearing side by side.

Still missing are Scribe Alowen, Ambassadorial Aide Soren, and the Alluran Princess, Ilya. Alluran and Bachhan officers are on the hunt. The Alluran monarchy and Bachhan mayoral office have each presented theories and suspicions on the responsible party behind these disappearances.

Alowen could only think about her mother and Uncle Rogan. How worried they must feel right now. It hurt to imagine.

Mr. Loggerman turned off the pixilator. "They haven't said anything outright yet, but rumors are already out there that Allurus thinks the Bachhan mayor and his son might be involved." He fiddled with the pixilator controller before setting it on a sturdy wooden table. He looked at them skeptically, keeping a wide distance. "Bachha says Allurus has no proof and it's trying to start a pointless fight." He faced them squarely with his hands on his hips. "And here are you three at my door. What is really going on here? Are you all trying to be funny?"

Soren and the princess turned to look at Alowen. She sighed and pulled her thoughts together a moment before turning to Mr. Loggerman.

"Both Bachha and Allurus are being turned upside down right now. Soren and I are from the Arbor, so they'll search there too. And you're"—she looked around the ranch's timber log walls and long, dark wood tables—"you're from home too. I just…" She shook her head. "This woman and her baby are in danger, and we have nowhere else to go."

There was silence. The princess and Soren looked at Mr. Loggerman. One minute passed, then another.

Finally, he rubbed his hairy neck and sighed. "I'll close shop for a few days. You three can stay here while you figure out what to do next. My washroom is four doors down the hall to the right. Dinner's cooking."

Later that same evening, Alowen set down her spoon with a sigh and leaned back in her chair. "Thank you, Mr. Loggerman. Seriously." Her back and legs still ached, but at least Loggerman's warm shower had helped.

"Don't make me regret this."

She couldn't blame him for being hesitant. Most people would have turned them away, or worse, called the authorities.

"Truly, sir, we can't thank you enough."

Across from her, Soren also looked rested. Still worn with ashy skin but at least rested. Next to her, the princess's plate was still half filled. Maybe it was the richness of Loggerman's roasted quail and creamy mashed potatoes that didn't agree with her. It was more than that though, of course. So much more.

"Princess Ilya?" Alowen slowly put her arm around the princess' shoulders. "How are you feeling?" No response. The princess had her gaze still on her plate. "I bet you aren't feeling great. I know you don't know me at all really, but I'm a good listener." Alowen gently rested her hand on the princess' forearm as she gripped her fork, motionless.

"Listen, maybe you are too tired right now to talk. I understand. I just want you to know I am here to listen whenever you are ready."

Slowly, the princess raised her face. She looked back at Alowen. Her eyes were full of tears as she lay forward on the table and buried her face in her arms.

Alowen pulled her chair closer and leaned in. "You've had a really hard time recently. This is a lot to deal with."

In the background, Mr. Loggerman cleared his throat and lifted some dishes off the table while Soren quietly lowered himself into the other chair next to Alowen, leaning in toward them with a concerned frown on his face.

Muffled sobs escaped the princess's arms. Alowen scooted her dinner plate away so Princess Ilya's hair wouldn't get in it.

"I know you are scared, but I promise we are going to keep you safe. We are going to figure this out, all of us."

She wasn't sure if she was lying, but they were going to do the best they could, she knew that at least. Slowly, the princess's sobs grew quieter. Soren sighed, gently passing a napkin to Alowen. Finally, the princess sat up and Alowen handed her the napkin. She dabbed her eyes and murmured a soft thanks.

"I've made some tea." Mr. Loggerman brought back a tea pot painted with red flowers on a wooden tray, the four teacups rattling a bit as he set it down. "Milk or sugar, Princess?" His thickly muscled hand looked funny holding such a dainty cup.

"No thank you, just the tea is fine," the princess whispered back.

"Careful, it's hot." He handed her the cup and sat at the end of the table. "Chamomile should help you sleep."

Soren stood, pouring himself and Alowen a cup. "We are in this together, you, me, Alowen, and the baby. We will find a safe place to hide until the baby comes."

The princess sat still for a while. Then she took a deep breath, straightening in her chair. "I think I'm ready to talk now."

They all kept silent as she swallowed and then began.

"I don't know how you know." She looked at Alowen. "But yes, I'm pregnant." She continued without looking up for reactions. "The baby belongs to Leiland, the Bachhan mayor's son. I know, we knew, that our relationship would be very discouraged. We never meant for it to go this far. We first met at an event in Bachha to raise money for the preservation of historic Alluran artifacts. In fact, our parents introduced us. I don't think it occurred to them there could be any attraction between us, and truthfully, at first there wasn't. But he is so warm, such a charismatic person." Her hand shook and the tea attempted to spill. She set the cup down and continued.

"We ran into each other again over the course of months at other community events. Eventually, the spark between us became too much to resist, despite my fear of repercussions. He dared anything, anything but drugs."

Soren looked across the table knowingly at Alowen. She couldn't imagine how much worse things could be if Leiland had relapsed.

"We began meeting more frequently, posing as friends. Things got out of hand, and we fell in love. We dreamed of a life together and made a plan to run away. When we realized I was pregnant, I got scared and cut things off. I tried to hide the pregnancy from my family, but of course, they figured it out." She put her hand on her stomach and rubbed her barely visible bump as though she were soothing the baby inside.

"My father was so angry, he locked me in a room and accused me of many things. He called me horrible names and threatened to disown me. He always suspected it was Lei's baby from all the time Lei and I had spent together, but he had no way to prove it. They kept me in that room for weeks so no one in Allurus could find out. But Lei never gave up on me. He had maids willing to sneak me messages leading up to the Party.

"He didn't do anything during Opening Night Procession so no one suspected, but he swapped me with another Alluran girl, a dancer, after the Closing Night Procession when security had their guard down. Things went the way he said they would, until they found her. I'm so worried about him. He promised he would take me to the surface, near the volcanoes. You all"—she gestured to Alowen and Soren—"you weren't supposed to be here. So, I know, I know in my heart, I know something bad happened."

They all sat in silence. This didn't feel like the right time to confess the guards had gotten Leiland. It was all too much. Soren shifted uncomfortably in his chair.

Finally, Mr. Loggerman got up. "You must be exhausted, princess. May I show you to your room? It's been a long day."

He stepped closer and she took his extended arm as she stood up shakily from the table. "Goodnight," she said meekly to Alowen and Soren.

"Sleep well."

"See you in the morning."

They watched him lead her away. Neither of them said

anything for a while.

"What a story, huh?" Soren finally asked.

Alowen nodded. All the dots finally connected from the past days. Heartbreaking. She couldn't imagine falling in love like that, knowing you could never be together in peace. Having to jump through so many hoops and plotting to run away from your lives and families, for love? It made her angry. Just because tradition states the Elements should remain separated doesn't make it right. It seemed outdated and cruel.

"Hey." Soren tapped his fingers on the table. "Can I ask you something?"

It was late, and she would really rather fall asleep and forget all of this for a few hours, but this was Soren. She owed it to him.

"Alright." Alowen crossed her arms and met his eyes. "What is it?"

"Why are you doing this? You could've walked away. You were just chosen as one of the scribes for the Party. You just finished days of interviewing with an elaborate list of celebrities." He let his hands flop on the table. "And you threw it all away. I don't understand. Why?"

She sat forward and took a deep breath. Finally, someone had asked the question she had been asking herself.

"You are probably going to think I am crazy. To be honest, I wondered at first too. I started having visions while we were in Wolken. Visions of the princess locked in that room. At first, I didn't understand what was happening. I didn't even know who she was. Then I saw her at the procession. I still wasn't sure. She looked fine that night. But I was so confused, you thought I was upset." She gave him a weak smile. "Remember?"

He nodded slowly.

"But then when all of this unfolded. I—knew about her

pregnancy. Maybe I knew." She closed her eyes, searching herself. Surprisingly, her mind was clear, without doubt. "I knew in my bones I was *supposed* to help her. Call it fate if you like, but it's the only thing that makes any sense to me." She closed her eyes waiting for him to call her crazy, to be angry with her.

"You aren't crazy, Alowen."

She opened her eyes again, surprised.

"My mom had visions like that too. A lot of people said she was crazy, but I knew they were real. Once, she had a vision that the bakery owner near our house was going to get very sick. She rushed there first thing in the morning and found him lying on the floor. They brought the doctor right away and the doctor said if she hadn't found him in time, well…"

"Wow. I never knew that about your mom. I bet she was so grateful to have a son like you who believed her."

Soren smiled softly. "Thank you. I miss her. All the time."

"What about you?" Alowen had been holding in her guilt all day. "You had a full, ambassadorial crew. It looked like your campaign was changing Allurus' reputation for the better. I'm sorry I made you leave all that. I'm sorry you had to abandon Sal to help me."

Soren's jaw grew tight. "It's not your fault," he murmured. "Ever since Sal started his political career advocating for more progressive ideals, asking the king to fund education and new technology over military budgets, they've always wanted a reason to bring him in. This would have happened either way. It's just"—he clenched his fist—"I just made him, and the rest of my crew, look guiltier by running."

"I'm sorry. I'm so sorry." Her eyes filled with tears.

"It's okay." Soren kept staring at the table. "Like I said,

it's not your fault. I was the one who chose this road."

"So…so why did you?"

Soren looked up at her. "I saw two frightened girls in front of me. I just reacted. I guess at the end of the day, I just had to do something. I don't know if I could have helped Sal, but looks like I managed to help you and the princess, huh?"

"You really did." She reached out and squeezed his fist. "Thank you, Soren." They sat there for a long while. Finally, Alowen got up. "Well, good night."

"Good night."

***

Alowen stood in a huge room with walls lined with square, glass openings and where water splashed gently. Some held empty orbs. Was this the Bachhan loading docks Merritt had told her about so many days ago? It must be the middle of the night judging by the dim light. For some reason, there was a camera mounted on a tripod pointed at a broad wall. A portal swirled on one end of the wall. She tried to move but couldn't. She looked down to see nothing, not her hands nor feet. She must be dreaming again.

A scuffle and muffled shouting erupted behind her. A group of guards dragged a gagged Leiland past her. He was writhing against them, but they were too strong, hauling him near the wall in front of the camera.

After some minutes, a sharply dressed Alluran official marched in through another door, followed by a Bachhan in a neat suit. Both were talking softly but then the Alluran kept walking forward and toward the camera while the Bachhan hung back.

When the Alluran entered the camera's frame, he nodded. "Start recording."

A green light blinked on the camera.

"Ladies and gentlemen of the Element," the man said. "I'm Lieutenant Arlott of Alluran Investigations. I'm sure you are all very confused by what you see now. Let me explain. Over twenty-four hours ago, our princess was abducted from her dressing room after the Closing Night Procession. Our armed forces have been on the hunt for her ever since our discovery. Unfortunately"—he looked coldly back at Leiland—"she is still at large." He paused. "In her place was a young girl who is here to confess what has happened."

Another soldier came into the room with a trembling girl, ushering her in front of the camera. Leiland protested through his gag, but a guard drew the cloth tighter, and he winced. His body pulsed with a bright red flame, casting an eerie, crimson glow across the room. The girl kept her gaze down.

"Please inform the Element what you have told us."

She swallowed and looked up through tears. "This man, the mayor's son, he convinced me to help smuggle the princess out of Allurus. Up to the surface. He said she was in danger."

"Thank you very much, that's enough." Lieutenant Arlott shifted her aside gently. "I understand the world has its differences with Allurus. We operate differently than the other Elements, it's true, but our laws and traditions offer us necessary protection and retribution for breaking them. We have no choice but to execute this young man for the crime of kidnapping our princess, whom we remind you all is still missing. She may even be dead as I speak."

Alowen wanted to yell the princess was alive, that they were making a mistake. She opened her mouth but couldn't make a sound.

"This may seem extreme but let me also remind you this crime was carried out against us and our princess with no provocation or regard for our sanctity. Allurus believes that harm done to one of us should be repaid with harm to the guilty. We cannot stop you from judging us, but please ask yourselves first, would your governments do the same for you? None of the other Elements pursue violence under any circumstances, yes, but will this nobility cost you your safety?"

He shook his head and turned to Leiland. "By decree of Allurus, you are being charged for abduction of a member of the Allurus Royal Family. You are sentenced to execution."

The guards tightened their grip. Leiland's eyes widened as the guards lowered his gag. His flame kept burning.

"If there is any justice, you will pay for this. You don't know how powerful my father is—"

One large guard placed his hand firmly over Leiland's mouth as they lowered him into the water inside the glass portal. His muffled cries leaked through the guard's fingers right before he swiftly snapped his neck like a chicken bone. There was an audible crack, and his body went limp. Alowen screamed, but nothing came out. The four guards hopped into the portal, and they dragged his body down into the water out of sight.

A red light flashed on the camera. It seemed to be off.

Lieutenant Arlott turned back to his Bachhan companion. "Things with Bachha will be completely flipped upside down now."

"We've talked about this." The other man said calmly. "Bachha will be occupied for a while. And it's about time. I'm no Alluran, but all Bachha ever does now is party. Our defenses and our politicians are a joke. It's time for Bachha to take itself seriously again."

The lieutenant looked admiringly at the camera. "Well, at least I thank you for this high-tech gift of yours. I did tell my superiors how allies inside Bachha would be useful one day."

The room faded to black.

Alowen sat up shaking. Her skin was damp with sweat yet somehow her body was cold. She jumped to her feet when she saw the yellow curtains framing the window and the cozy quilted chair in the corner, then took a deep breath. Oh yes, she forgot. They were at Mr. Loggerman's house.

It was more than a dream, no point in denying it. She walked to the window, cracking it open to feel cool air on her skin. As the beads of sweat began to dry, she closed her eyes and wrapped her arms around her shivering shoulders. If Leiland was gone… She shuddered. Relations between the Elements were always fragile, but for over a century now, things had been stable. If Allurus had just executed Leiland, what would that mean? Would Bachha and Allurus go to war? It was still dark outside, and the stars were high in the sky. She could see her favorite constellation, the Archer and his bow. She used to make wishes on it as a child.

Suddenly she was overcome, sobs wracking her body. She lay back on the bed, heaving, hoping the noise wouldn't wake anyone, but she couldn't hold back. She longed for home. She wanted to be in her bed in her mom's house with Uffy tucked under her chin. She wanted the familiar smells of her mother's biscuits in the mornings and stew in the evenings and the sound of the crackling fire. More than anything she wanted to erase yesterday's events. For better or worse, she was in this now, and she couldn't get out.

***

The sun was almost up to the tree line when Alowen stumbled to the dining area bleary eyed. She was somehow exhausted and wide awake simultaneously. How could she tell her cohorts about her vision of Leiland? How would the poor princess take it? She flinched when she saw everyone already at the table. Soren and the princess looked worn too. Mr. Loggerman must have a niece or daughter because the princess seemed to be wearing casual hand-me-down clothes. The pixilator droned softly on the wall, but no one was really watching it.

"Good morning, Alowen. How did you sleep?" Mr. Loggerman nodded gruffly.

He slid a plate of muffins bursting with red berries toward her. She sat down slowly, steadying herself with the table and grabbed a large muffin.

"To be honest, not well."

Soren looked up at her. "Sorry to hear, I slept like a rock." He hid his mouthful of muffin with a hand.

"I had another vision. A dream, but it wasn't a dream."

Soren stared, suddenly rapt and tense, and the princess looked up at her.

"You know," laughed Mr. Loggerman, "you are not the first person to report weird dreams in this house. Must be something about being out in the country." He put a pat of butter on a muffin and stuffed a giant bite in his mouth.

"Princess, I have to explain something to you, and it's going to sound crazy." The table stopped. "The reason… the way I knew you were pregnant; it was because I'd been having visions. I kept seeing you in that room where you were being held. I didn't believe it at first, but then I saw you at the procession and well, everything that has happened since."

"Oh." The princess looked back down at her plate. She didn't seem to have much energy. "I see. No wonder you already knew. It all makes sense." She looked uneasily at Alowen and crossed her arms protectively around her waist.

Mr. Loggerman lifted a large finger, looking unconvinced. "I tell you what Alowen, you have quite an imagination. You know, I used to like to tell stories when I was your age."

"It wasn't imagination," Soren snapped.

Mr. Loggerman looked at him quizzically.

"Thank you, Soren." It was kind of him to say, but she didn't blame Mr. Loggerman for not believing her. She barely believed herself at first. "I understand why you wouldn't believe me, Mr. Loggerman. It's a lot to take in—"

Her eye caught the pixilator. What was this? Leiland's face was onscreen.

"Everyone! Look! It's Leiland, can you please turn up the volume, Mr. Loggerman?"

The princess was already taking deep breaths, wide eyes fixated on the pixilator, straining to hear.

A newscaster's voice came out.

The search for the Alluran princess continues as Alluran forces have captured her accused abductor, the Bachhan mayor's son, Leiland. The footage we have obtained is…graphic in nature, please be advised.

Mr. Loggerman's face was white as a ghost. Soren stood up and moved closer to the screen. His hand gripped the top of a chair so tightly his fingers turned pale. Alowen glanced at the princess to see her rubbing her hand in small, rapid circles on her stomach. She shifted closer to her and held her breath, waiting for what she knew was coming. In a minute, the princess was going to need comfort.

The princess finally burst into tears when Leiland's flame blazed. Alowen wrapped her arms tight around her. As little as they knew each other, she was all the princess had right now. Her and Soren. The screen shifted to the Alluran lieutenant.

...our laws and traditions offer us necessary protection, and retribution for breaking them. We have no choice but to execute this young man for the crime of kidnapping our princess, whom we remind you all is still missing. She may even be dead as I speak.

"I can't bear it!" The princess ran from the dining hall.

Alowen looked to Soren, but he was already heading after her.

...Allurus believes that harm done to one of us should be repaid with harm to the guilty. We cannot stop you from judging us, but please ask yourselves first, would your governments do the same for you? None of the other elements pursue violence under any circumstances, yes, but will this nobility cost you your safety?

Mr. Loggerman didn't move. He kept his gaze right on the screen, a big hand cupping his chin.

The next scene is too graphic for pixilator content, but our organization can confirm the mayor's son has been executed.

Alowen's stomach dropped. A wave of nausea hit her. Even though her dream had shown her, now the reality set in. Leiland was gone. This would mean the search for Ilya would ramp up. She had to get them to safety somewhere, and fast.

Mr. Loggerman switched off the pixilator, loudly clearing his throat.

"I should go check on them," Alowen said, her voice

cracking.

Mr. Loggerman nodded, leaning forward into the table. "There will be quite an outrage back in Bachha, no doubt. This has caused a lot of tension between the Allurus and Bachhans. Perhaps not outright war, not right away, but the storm's brewing fast. Now then, we need to get you kids moving soon. They will be looking for you, even more now."

Alowen nodded. "You are right. Time is short."

She turned for the door and found them just outside the door near the pasture. The princess was sitting on a stool, tears streaming down her face.

"This is all my fault! How could I let this happen?"

"This was not your fault, Princess. People don't choose to fall in love. It just happens."
It felt like a weak argument, but she couldn't let those words hang in the room with no response.

"What am I going to do now? What are we going to do?" The princess placed her hand gently onto her stomach.

Alowen's heart broke for her. "For now, we need to find a place for you to be safe until the baby is born. Soren and I are working on it, right?"

Soren's face was full of trepidation when he looked back at her. "Yes, I have some ideas of where we can go. I don't know how we will get there though. Our goose has flown away. "He looked grimly into the distance. "We'd better get back inside. We can't risk being seen."

Alowen helped the princess back indoors, holding her steady. She was shivering slightly, so she wrapped it her own scarf around Princess Ilya's shoulders.

Inside, Mr. Loggerman was furiously scrubbing the table with a rag. "I can offer you one of my eagles and some supplies." He fixed his eyes on Alowen. "Stay another night or two. But the sooner you get going, the safer you will be. They may have tracked you here." He scratched his beard.

"I'm sorry, I wish I had more to offer you kids than a few nights stay."

"I understand." Alowen had expected this. "We appreciate everything you have done for us, truly. We will take you up on the eagle, and I will find a way to repay you. I promise."

"That won't be necessary. Just get through this in one piece, you hear me?" His look almost seemed apologetic. "Allurus is still hunting you."

Something else came to mind. "All this was in my dream—and I remember now. There was a Bachhan there with Lieutenant Arlott. He said Bachha would be occupied for a while, that it's time for things to change."

"Well." Mr. Loggerman shrugged. "Dream or not, it's true. Some Bachhans will want war with Allurus, but I bet there are others who feel the Allurans were justified, even within their council. Bachha will find itself stalled with indecision, for now." He cracked his neck. "But one thing's for sure. Some Bachhans will hunt you now too. If they can get to the princess before Allurus, they might use her to get vengeance for the mayor's son."

Alowen swallowed. She hadn't thought about that.

Soren cleared his voice. "There is a lot of unexplored area in the Arbor to the west. It's sparsely populated. I think if we take enough supplies, we could hide there for a while. It might take a couple of days by eagle. We will probably have to stop and rest a few times, but I think we can make it."

It sounded like a good plan. It was either this or the empty hill ranges that Wolken hadn't expanded to yet.

"Okay, let's go," the princess spoke. "But first, there is one more thing I should tell all of you." The room got quiet again as she stood and carefully lifted her shirt. Just above her navel was a metallic blue sigil against her pale green skin, like a tattoo. The phases of the moon wound clockwise around a series of other markings. It was that same sigil on Dexran's book cover.

"Is that, is that the sigil? From The Frozen Years?" Alowen's blood ran cold.

Soren sucked in his breath and Mr. Loggerman frowned.

"It is. One morning early in the pregnancy, it just showed up on my skin." The princess traced the sigil. "It's been growing clearer each week."

Suddenly it all came rushing in. Alowen's skin was on fire. This was the baby, the baby from the legend she'd grown up hearing about. This was the mixed Element child that was going to save them from another freeze.

Adenike's words echoed, *You'll learn to balance that pressure with patience and compassion. This world is brand new for you. In time, it'll feel like an old glove, and you'll walk into any room confidently. But for now, it's okay to acknowledge this is scary!*

She closed her eyes and took a deep breath. A calm knowing spread through her body.

Alowen smiled softly. "Let's pack our things and then rest here one more night. We will head out in the morning." They could do this. They had to. She grabbed Soren's and the princess' hands, squeezing both gently. "We are going to get through this"—she took a deep breath—"Together."

Thank you

I would like to acknowledge the support and encouragement of my sober community without whom this work would have never seen the light of day. I would also like to thank my editor and publisher for their guidance and expertise in bringing this story to life. Finally, I am grateful to my readers for their enthusiasm and passion for the fantastical world I have created.

Thank you for embarking on this adventure with me.

About Natalie Brougham

Natalie grew up worshipping fiction and fiction writers like Roald Dahl, Douglas Adams, and Kurt Vonnegut. On many occasions she was in big trouble for reading all night as a child instead of sleeping, but that never stopped her. Fiction has been a sufficient substitute for reality on occasions when reality wasn't cooperating. Natalie has been writing her entire life and has other completed works she hopes to publish. Natalie lives in Michigan with her daughter Annabelle, and her two cats; Bixy and Snax.

Wild Ink Publishing is new to the publishing industry, which means we are able to showcase some of the brightest wordsmiths by unleashing the shackles that usually stop people from publishing traditionally.

wild-ink-publishing.com

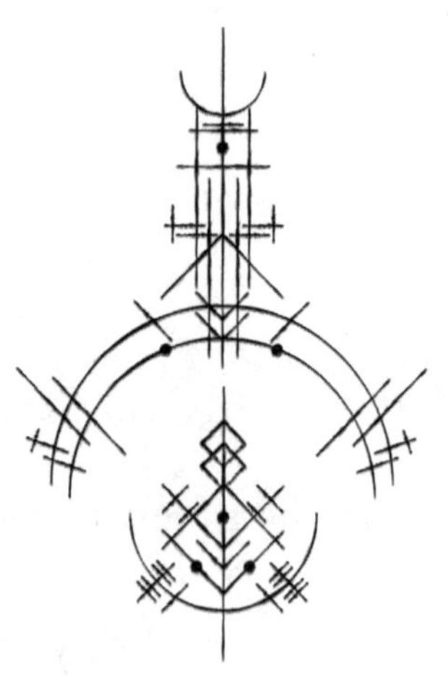

www.ingramcontent.com/pod-product-compliance
Lightning Source LLC
Chambersburg PA
CBHW020812190726
48285CB00006B/2253